THE PERILS OF POLLY

Just as war is threatening in 1939, Dr Lena Turner's grandmother asks her to find Polly, her friend from fifty years ago. Lena finds herself in Cariastan, where she meets handsome Gregori, grandson of the Countess for whom Polly had been a lady's maid. Lena is swept into a story of mystery, romance and danger — but will she also be swept off her feet by Gregori?

First published in Great Britain in 2021

First Linford Edition
published 2022

*A catalogue record for this book is available
from the British Library.*

ISBN 978–1–4448–4935–6

Published by
Ulverscroft Limited
Anstey, Leicestershire

Printed and bound in Great Britain by
TJ Books Ltd., Padstow, Cornwall

This book is printed on acid-free paper

SALLY QUILFORD

◆

THE PERILS
OF POLLY

Complete and Unabridged

LINFORD
Leicester

1

London was preparing for war, which they had been told was only weeks away. Already sandbags lined all municipal buildings and the entrances to the tube. The atmosphere in Britain was part anticipation, part fear. ARC wardens stood on every corner, primed and ready for when their time came to guide everyone to safety.

Lena deftly stepped around them, her heels making a rhythmic sound on the pavement as she came up out of the Trafalgar Square tube and began walking up the Mall. She might have been just a pretty fair-haired, brown eyed girl in a yellow sundress, yet heads turned when she passed by, because of her confidence. What might have been brief glances became lingering looks because of the dimples in her cheeks, which gave an impression of humour mixed with intelligence.

The Cariastan Embassy, an opulent white Georgian Villa, was set among trees and elegant gardens. Lena showed her card to the sentry and was quietly ushered up to the front door.

'Doctor Turner,' she told the concierge. 'I have an appointment to see the Countess.' He led her into an ornate marble hallway, with a sweeping central staircase, and told her to wait.

A few minutes later, a man walked down the stairs, as an actor walking into the screen. He was devastatingly handsome, olive skinned, and dressed in a grey lounge suit. He had thick, dark wavy hair, and his eyes were very nearly black.

'Doctor Turner?' he said, frowning. Lena did not have to be told that he was expecting a man. People usually did.

'That is correct. And you are.'

'Gregori de Luca. The Countess is my grandmother. Could I speak to you in private for a moment?' He gestured towards an oak door to the side of the hallway. 'I would like to ask you a few questions before I take you to my grandmother's room.'

'Of course,' Lena said. She had nothing to hide, even though the formality of the situation unnerved her. She followed him through the door, into a small study. There was a sofa in front of a fireplace. The fire was not lit. Already, people were preserving coal.

'Please, sit down.' Gregori gestured to the sofa. Lena sat down, but he did not. He stood with his back to the fireplace. 'Before we go any further, I want to explain to you that my grandmother is very old and frail now, and she is still recovering from our escape from Europe.'

He spoke English perfectly, but there was a faint trace of an Eastern European accent. 'Unfortunately, my grandfather is still over there, and every day we fear for his safety. So, you will understand that I do not want her to be distressed in any way.'

'Of course, and it is not my intention

to distress her. In fact, I come because of my own grandmother. She knows your grandmother. She watched her grow up.'

'Is that so?'

'Yes, at Derwent Priory, in Derbyshire, where your grandmother, who was Clara Harrington at the time, lived as a girl.'

'Ah . . . Yes, I see.' His eyes were watchful.

'My grandmother is also very old and frail now,' Lena explained. 'She's in her nineties. Lately, she has spoken a lot about another young woman who worked at the Priory. This young woman, Polly Smith, was your grandmother's maid. I was named after her — Paulina, though I go by Lena. Sorry, er . . . Count . . .' Lena realised she did not know how to address him.

'It's just Mr de Luca here, but please call me Greg. The older generation have all these protocols about names and titles, but I prefer to think that we can speak as equals. If not, why are we about to go to war against a tyrant?'

'I keep hoping we won't go to war, even at this late stage. Is that naïve of me?'

'A little, but it's good to be hopeful. You were talking about this Polly?'

'Yes, as I said, Polly was Miss Clara's . . . your grandmother's maid. My Nana, Bessie Cooper, thought of Polly as a daughter. Miss Clara left to go to Cariastan to marry your grandfather, taking Polly with her, but although Polly wrote to my Nana regularly at first, after a few weeks, the letters just stopped coming. Nana wrote to the Countess and got a very nice reply about how Polly had moved on to a new employer but . . .'

'But what?'

'Nana doesn't believe Polly would have done that. She was devoted to Miss Clara. I hope it's not presumptuous of me to say that they were like sisters.'

'Are you suggesting that my grandmother lied?'

Lena blushed. 'No, of course not. Nana just wants to know what happened to Polly, because she hasn't heard from

5

her for nearly fifty years and she thinks of her all the time lately. I thought that if I could just find out where Polly went, after leaving your grandmother, I could set Nana's mind at rest that her friend has had a long and happy life.'

'Does she have any reason to think that might not be the case?'

Greg's question surprised Lena, because it seemed as if he already knew why they were so concerned. He had been on guard from the moment she mentioned Polly's name.

If he did know the reason, what did that mean? Could she even trust him? She told herself she was being silly. Whatever happened was fifty years ago, long before they were born. The past did not concern either of them, other than Lena's wish to bring peace to her much-loved grandmother's life. She took a deep breath and told him, 'Just before Polly left for Cariastan, there was an attempt on her life.'

2

1890

Polly danced around the kitchen. 'Not long now, Mrs Cooper. My first trip abroad with Miss Clara.' She was a twenty-two-year-old ball of energy, with flaming auburn hair, her face covered in freckles.

'You settle yourself down,' Bessie Cooper said, tutting and rolling her eyes. 'You'll do yourself an injury. You'll do *me* an injury, if you don't stand still while I stir this stew!'

Bessie was thirty-eight years old, with mousy brown hair and a round, honest face. She had given over twenty years of her life to Derwent Priory. Not because she liked her master and mistress, but because she saw herself as the protector of every young girl who was unlucky enough to enter the place as a servant. Or as the orphaned daughter of the original owners, for that matter.

Bessie screeched as Polly grabbed her and waltzed her around the big oak table, where the staff ate their meals and Bessie created her masterpieces for the people upstairs. Laughing, Bessie extricated herself and went back to stirring the pot of stew on the stove. It was the staff supper, and needed to be ready and put aside before she even started on the family meals. That night they had a very important dinner party, and Bessie wanted it to be perfect, if only for Miss Clara's sake.

'They say Cariastan is beautiful, Mrs Cooper. It has castles, palaces, churches, synagogues, mosques. And everyone speaks English, because Queen Victoria's second cousin eight times removed went there to become king, or something. Pity though, I would have liked to learn a different language. Like French maybe.'

'Language learning is not for the likes of us, Polly. It's for people like Miss Clara. Now she would sound lovely in French.

You, well, you'd still have that Derbyshire accent. Talking of Miss Clara, you'd better go and get her ready for dinner. The guests will be arriving soon.'

Polly kissed Bessie's cheek. They had known each other since Polly first came to work at Derwent Priory as a twelve-year-old. She had come from an orphanage and was shy and terrified of her new boss, Bessie Cooper. Bessie, for her part, had immediately melted at the sadness in the little girl's green eyes, but tried hard to hide it with the professionalism expected from her employers. It did not last long. The first time little Polly had a nightmare, it was Bessie who held her in her arms and soothed her back to sleep with a lullaby.

'You'll not think of me when you're gone off to Cariawotsit,' Bessie said now.

'I'll never forget you, Mrs Cooper. And we'll come back to visit. Miss Clara is only moving countries. Not to the moon.'

'What's happening here?' The butler, Mr Turner entered the kitchen. He was a tall, thin man of about fifty, with distinguished grey hair and icy eyes. 'Aren't you supposed to be helping Miss Clara get dressed?' he snapped at Polly. 'And you, Mrs Cooper, there's a dinner to be cooked.'

'You don't tell me how to do my job and I shan't tell you how to do yours,' Bessie told him. She was the only person who dared speak to him in that tone. 'And leave my girls alone too. Barking at them all day long.'

'Now, Mrs Cooper,' he said. 'They know I don't mean anything by it. I just don't want them getting into trouble with Mr Harrington.'

Polly, who had never lost her fear of Mr Turner, and had never thought he did not mean anything by his shouting, crept out. She took the back stairs to the west wing of the priory. None of the building was warm, as the family had been reluctant to spend money on mod cons, but the back stairs were particularly chilly, because they saw no sunlight at all.

The other maids were bustling along

the corridors, frantically ensuring the rooms were ready for the expected guests. The plan was that they would arrive at five o'clock, be shown to their rooms, then dinner would be served. It was now four o'clock, and last-minute plans were in place, with fires lit, warm towels placed and a spot check by Mrs Jenkins, the housekeeper, to ensure not a spot of dust remained.

'You're cutting it fine,' Mrs Jenkins said to Polly. She stood with her arms folded, the keys to the priory hanging from a chain on her waist. She resembled an early Christian martyr, but her bark was worse than her bite. 'She hasn't had her bath yet.'

'She's got hours.'

'Yes, but you know what she's like when she drifts off into a dream world. Honestly, I think a puff of wind would blow that girl away.'

Polly found Miss Clara Harrington sitting in front of her dressing table mirror, staring into space. Clara was the quintessential English Rose, with hair the colour of corn and huge blue eyes set in a peaches and cream complexion. Because of her looks, people had a habit of underestimating her, but Polly knew that there could be steel in Clara's spine. She was looking at a pile of papers, flicking through the pages.

'Are you ready for your bath, Miss Clara?' Polly asked.

'No . . .' Clara turned and stood up, then ran into Polly's arms, crying. 'Oh Polls! Whatever am I to do?'

Polly deftly kicked the bedroom door shut, in case one of the other servants saw. 'It's alright, pet,' she said stroking Clara's hair. 'It'll work out fine. They say that your cousin, the Count is very handsome.'

'Will that matter if he's cruel and beats me?'

'I won't let that happen!' Polly protested. 'You're my best friend.' She lowered her voice. Mrs Jenkins was always telling her off about getting ideas about her station, but she and Clara had been friends since she arrived from the orphanage. They had both been lonely children and they found solace with each other. 'But there's no reason to think he will. He's been very kind about everything so far.'

'Why can't I marry who I like? Or even not marry at all.'

'We've talked about this. When you marry, your money will be all yours and your aunt and uncle won't be able to tell you what to do ever again.'

'No,' said Clara, pulling away and slumping back down in her chair. 'My husband will instead. Have you read this contract? It's full of my list of duties as a Countess, and as a wife. I have to give him at least two children to carry on the line. I have to give him half of my inheritance . . . But he does say it will go into trust for our children, which I suppose is what my mother did for me. If he keeps his promise, that is. There's nothing to say he will.'

'But he can't touch the rest of your money, so you'll be able to do whatever you want.'

'I'm going to create an orphanage, run by kind non-judgemental people, so that no child ever has to be as unhappy as you and I were. I'll help to teach them to read and write, like I did with you. And you can help too, so they have all the skills they need, not just to clean other people's grates, but to go into clerical work, or even better.'

'See? You have it all worked out,' said Polly. 'I shall be at your side all the way.'

'Yes, I'm so glad I stood up to Uncle John about that. He was so certain you should stay here. I'm sure the staff in Cariastan are very nice, but I will have to be all formal with them.'

'So, shall I prepare your bath now?'

'Yes, I suppose so, then. You always cheer me up, Polls.'

'It's what I am here for,' Polly replied.

'I think it's very silly that we can't be friends in public as well as in private. One day, people won't care about such things.'

'But they do now, Pet, so we have to be careful. If I lose my job, I can't come with you.'

Clara's face darkened again. 'Oh, don't say that. Don't even joke about such a thing. Quick, draw my bath, before I change my mind again. Please,' she remembered to add. Clara might have taught Polly to read and write, but Polly had taught Clara that you should always say please and thank you.

Two hours later, Clara was ready, dressed in a blue satin dress with a bustle at the back. Her fair hair was piled high on her hair, and her fringe had been teased into tight curls. 'Like Princess Alexandra,' Polly smiled.

'I'll buy you new clothes when I have my own money,' Clara promised.

'I can buy my own clothes,' Polly said, gently but firmly. She made it a rule never to accept anything from Clara, apart from the occasional second-hand day dress that Clara did not wear anymore. None of Clara's ballgowns fit into Polly's lifestyle anyway.

'Then promise me that one day I might buy your wedding dress.'

'It's a deal.'

'I shall find you a nice duke.'

Polly laughed. 'Dukes don't marry ladies' maids.'

'Then they're fools.' Clara kissed Polly on the cheek. 'Because you really are the best.'

Clara left the room, her head held high, so that her Aunt Mabel and Uncle John would not know that she had been afraid. Whatever she shared with Polly, to them she always put on a brave face.

Polly picked up the clothes that Clara had strewn on the floor and sorted through them. There were petticoats to be mended, and a greasy spot to be cleaned from the dress that Clara had worn at lunch that day. She would take it down to the servants' hall, where there was an ironing board and greaseproof paper, along with a sewing kit for the petticoats.

John and Mabel Harrington had allowed Clara access to her trust fund for some new clothes for her trip to Cariastan, but they had insisted that for the most part she wore the clothes she already had. Many were old, but Polly's deft way with a needle made them look like new again.

After making sure the room was tidy, Polly gathered up the clothes to be tended to, and opened the door to the hallway.

She walked slap bang into one of the tallest men she had ever seen, knocking the clothes from his arms and those from her own, so they landed in a homogenous heap on the floor.

'Oh, soz,' she said, in the slang she used with all the other servants.

He looked at her and smiled, speaking in a strange, but very alluring accent. 'Soz? What is this soz?' He was dressed in a valet's outfit, with thick dark curly hair and nearly black eyes. His skin was olive toned, suggesting Italian or Greek origin.

'Sorry, I meant. Did you come with the visitors?'

'Yes, I am Anton, valet to the Ambassador Lorenzo.'

They knelt down together to untangle the mess of clothing. 'I was looking for somewhere to iron the ambassador's shirt. They tell me the back stairs are this way and that I must not use the grand staircase. The man called Turner shouted at me.'

'I'll bet he did,' Polly laughed. 'Do you do things differently in Cariastan?'

'I suppose we do. I have not thought about it until now.'

'You can follow me. I'm Polly, maid to Miss Clara. As you can see, I was just on my way to the same place.'

Anton held up a petticoat. 'This, I think, is yours?'

'No, that's Miss Clara's,' Polly quipped, taking them from him. 'Mine cost much more than that.'

He frowned, then smiled, as if realising the joke, and Polly thought her heart might just stop. There were always handsome footmen or valets coming and going from the Priory. They did not last long, on account that Mr Harrington did not approve of what he called shenanigans among the staff. He did not seem to mind having pretty girls around quite as much. Anton was a cut above the usual handsome jack the lad who had worked there and left a trail of broken hearts behind. She decided it was the accent. He was probably quite plain without it. Stick a Derbyshire accent on him and he probably looked like a troll. She stopped, realising that she was actually staring at him beyond what was normal.

'I'll show you to the servants' hall.' She led him to the staircase at the far end of the hallway. 'This is the one we use. Are you new to England? Do they really let servants use the main staircase in Cariastan? We can only use the backstairs, unless we're cleaning the main staircase. Is it very beautiful there?'

'Yes. I do not think so, but I am nervous here and forget. And yes. It is very beautiful,' Anton said, with an amused tone in his voice.

'You'll have to forgive me,' Polly said, descending the stairs. 'I always talk a lot when I am nervous and excited. I am so looking forward to seeing Cariastan, and I want to know all about it. I hope you can spare some time to tell me.'

'I shall be delighted to, Miss Polly.'

'Not Miss Polly. Just Polly. Only ladies get called Miss. And Mrs Jenkins and Mrs Cooper are always Mrs, even though they're not married. Don't worry, Anton. I'll teach you about England and you can tell me about Cariastan.'

'And this Miss Clara? Is she a good person?'

'She's the sweetest person you could ever meet. And really beautiful. If your Count doesn't fall in love with her at first sight, then there must be something wrong with him.'

'What if he sees someone else that he believes is just as beautiful? What if his heart suddenly beats for someone else?'

Polly stopped and turned to look at him. He was a couple of steps above her, so looked taller than ever. She gulped, but was determined not to be dominated by him.

'Look, I don't know what this Count

of yours got up to so far. That's his business, him being a man and all that. But he'd better be good to Miss Clara. She knows he might not love her and she not him, but he'd best treat her with respect.'

'Or he will have you to deal with, yes?' Anton said, his eyes twinkling.

'Absolutely.'

'She is lucky to have such a champion.'

'You must promise not to tell him I said all this. He might send me home and she needs a friend with her.'

'I shall not tell the Count anything. I cross my heart and hope to die. I think this is what you English say, yes?'

'That's the one.'

'I think that you and I are going to be good friends, Polly.'

She turned away, and started off down the stairs, so he could not see her blush.

'Now don't you go getting any ideas. I've seen off better men than you.'

It was a lie. None of the male servants had ever been better than Anton, and few had shown her any interest, often thinking she had ideas above her station, but he did not know any of that.

'I do not doubt it. With that hair, I think you were Boudicca in a previous life. I would be too afraid to cross you.'

He was teasing her, but she rather liked the image of herself, leading an army into battle.

With each step she took, she said a silent mantra . . . *Whatever you do, don't fall in love with the handsome valet.*

3

As Polly showed Anton around the servants' hall, Clara was in the drawing room with her aunt and uncle, awaiting their guests.

'Is that your new dress?' her aunt asked her.

'Yes, Aunt Mary.'

'It is rather more figure hugging than I expected. You do know you're not marrying the Ambassador?'

However nervous Clara was in her own room, she always tried to behave stronger in the company of her aunt and uncle. 'No, I am not, but he will be reporting back to my future husband, so it is important to create a good impression.'

'Humph. I am not sure you are. John, what do you think?'

'I think it hardly matters, under the circumstances.'

'What?' Aunt Mary blanched, then

nodded. 'No, perhaps not. Perhaps not. Clara, when you go to bed, I want you to tell Polly to come and see me in the garden room when she has finished with her duties. I need to have a word with her before you leave.'

'It will be very late, Aunt Mary. Can it not wait until tomorrow? Polly will be tired.'

Her aunt glared at her. 'We pay her a wage to be available at our convenience, and it is convenient for me to see her then. Her feelings do not come into the matter.'

'Might I remind you,' Clara said quietly, 'that I am the one who pays her salary, as I do all the staff here. We already have a turnover of staff unseen in other houses, because of the conditions here. Only a few stalwarts stick it out, like Mrs Jenkins, Mrs Cooper, Mr Turner and Polly. The former three stay, I think, because of my mother and father, whom they loved dearly, and I think I am not presumptuous in saying that they have the same love for me. I hope that when I am gone to Cariastan, you will be kinder to them, especially if I am to keep paying their salaries even after I am married.'

Uncle John stood up, and caught Clara by the arm, his fingers digging deeply into her soft flesh. 'Now you listen here, young lady. The bulk of the money might have gone to you, because of some pre-marital clause that your mother conned my dear departed brother into signing, but the Priory is my ancestral home, and I make the decisions as to who stays and who goes. I can, if I wish, send all those people you mentioned away tomorrow without a reference, insuring they are never employed again. Your aunt has politely asked you to ensure Polly Smith goes to see her later tonight. You will pass on that message, or your beloved servants will find themselves without a home and a job.'

Clara bit back the tears. She would not cry in front of them.

She had never told Polly of the exact nature of the cruelty she had suffered at the hands of her aunt and uncle. Of the million sly insults or subtle physical assaults that were hidden by supposed hand holding or even hugging, while threats of further violence, or causing pain to those below stairs that she loved, were whispered in her ear. Her aunt and uncle were always careful, even in front of the staff.

She was always afraid that her Polly would fly up the stairs and try to take them on. Her warrior friend would not win, because no matter how much she tried, Clara never truly won. She might have her inheritance, but until she married, she could not touch it, and as a young woman under twenty-one, she did not have the freedom to go where she pleased or do what she pleased.

'Yes, Uncle,' she said. 'I will do as you ask in order to keep the peace until I leave. But I promise you that if I have to take them all to Cariastan with me, I will. They won't need references with me, because I know their worth.'

John Harrington released his grip and laughed. 'That will be your husband's decision. I daresay he has much better servants than the lazy bumpkins who eat all my leftover beef and drink all my port dregs.'

'My beef. My port,' Clara muttered, well aware that she was being petty, but her uncle was not listening by then, because at that moment the doors opened and Turner stood there, ready to introduce the first batch of guests. They were mainly local landowners, and the vicar, Reverend Underwood.

'Here she is,' Aunt Mary said, smiling widely. 'Our beautiful girl, all grown up and ready to leave us to marry. My heart breaks to think of it.'

'You will miss her,' the Reverend said. 'But she will be a married woman, and you need not worry for her future.'

'It has been a worry,' said Aunt Mary, putting her arm around Clara's waist. Clara fought the compulsion to shrug her off. 'When we took her in, after dear Christian and Vivien passed away, we had no idea how to bring up a child. Now, we can wave her off as a young woman on the cusp of life, safe in the knowledge that we have done our Christian duty. She has been raised with love and in the end, that is all that matters, surely.'

The room was filled with 'aws', and various eyes dabbed with lace hankies, while Clara just felt nauseous. She had been raised by loving servants, and any Christianity her aunt laid claim to was of the worst kind, which had nothing to do with Christ and His kindness.

The next time Turner opened the door, he introduced a woman dressed all in black. 'Mrs Lovett.' She had waves of black hair on her head, that Clara suspected was a wig, and she appeared to be wearing rouge and lipstick, which drew murmurs from the other guests. Mrs Lovett swept into the room like a ship in full sail.

'Welcome, Mrs Lovett,' said John Harrington, stepping forward and extending his hand. 'I cannot tell you how grateful my wife and I are that you will be taking care of Clara for us until her marriage. Clara, dearest, come and meet your chaperone.'

'How do you do?' Clara said, politely. 'It is kind of you to take on this role. I don't think we've met yet . . .'

'We have not, dear,' said Mrs Lovett, with a smile. 'I can already tell that you and I are going to be great friends. I will be watchful, but not forbidding. I understand the young.'

That set Clara's mind at rest a little, even though she knew well enough not to trust what people said in public, compared to how they behaved in private. 'How do you know my aunt and uncle?'

'Oh, we met years ago, when they were on their honeymoon. My dear husband was alive then.'

'It was not long after that we took our darling Clara in,' Aunty Mary cut in. 'How time flies. Well, I think we are only awaiting the ambassador, and then we can eat. Would you like to go to your room and refresh, Mrs Lovett?'

'Thank you, but I stopped at a nearby inn to change, because I was so eager to spend time with my beautiful young charge.

I believe my luggage has been taken to my room, thanks to the estimable Turner. What a handsome man he is. I wonder that you do not worry he will break your female visitors' hearts, Mr Harrington.'

'It never occurred to me.'

The door opened and Turner appeared with someone whom Clara immediately mistook for the Prince of Wales. He was a man of about sixty with a fine, pointed beard, dressed in white, with dozens of medals on his chest, and a purple sash. His eyes twinkled on an intelligent face.

'Ambassador Lorenzo,' Turner announced.

'Good evening, dear man.' John Harrington stepped forward and made all the introductions, ending with Clara. 'And this is the young lady you have come to escort to Cariastan, Miss Clara Harrington, my niece.'

'How do you do, child? Your cousin, the Count de Luca has told me to express his wish that you are with him soon, so that he may drink in your beauty with his own eyes.'

'If you write to him before we leave, please thank him for me, and tell him I look forward to meeting him,' Clara said.

It could not be further from the truth. With the arrival of Mrs Lovett and the ambassador, who seemed to be decent enough people, the reality of her situation hit her. She might not have been happy at Derwent Priory since her mother and father had died in tragic circumstances, but it had been her home for over twenty years.

'You understand, Miss Harrington, when you have signed the contract after dinner tonight, that under Cariastan law the betrothal is legal and binding, and cannot be broken off by either party.'

'Yes, I understand.'

'There is the matter of a marriage in the eyes of the Lord,' Mrs Harrington said. 'Under British law, she will not be legally married until then. With that in mind, Mrs Lovett will remain as her chaperone, sleeping in her room if necessary, until the church marriage takes place.'

'Of course,' the ambassador bowed, 'And that ceremony will take place a couple of weeks after Miss Harrington's arrival in Cariastan. You have my solemn word that I will also protect her honour in this regard.'

Clara swallowed hard. She felt like a racehorse, being discussed for the Derby. She was surprised they did not check her teeth and flanks. She stifled a bout of hysterical laughter, determined to tell Polly about it all when they were alone.

'Shall we go into dinner?' John Harrington said. 'Then you can tell us more about our future nephew-in-law, Ambassador.'

Clara took the reverend's arm, and followed the others into the dining room, feeling less like a racehorse and more like a condemned prisoner going for her last meal.

★ ★ ★

A few hours later, Polly made her way down to the garden room. There was only one entrance that the servants could use, and it meant walking around the terrace and in through French doors. It had been raining, so the bottom of her dress was damp.

She was dog-tired, but could not ignore a direct command from Mrs Harrington, even if Clara had phrased it as gently as she could.

'You think I don't know,' she told Clara as she left her tucked up in bed. 'You think I don't understand what they are really like with you and how you fight for us. We all know and we all love you for it. But they're not always as discreet as they think. You don't know how many times I have stopped myself from flying down those stairs and telling them what I really think. What stopped me is that I know they'd send me away and then I wouldn't be able to help you. Then it might have been worse for you and I won't let that happen.'

'God bless you, Polly,' Clara said, her voice thick with emotion. 'We will be free soon, then you can stay with me till we're both old and grey.'

'You speak for yourself. I'm staying young forever.' Polly winked and Clara smiled through damp eyes.

'You always make me feel better. Thank you, my friend.'

The Priory rose above Polly, silhouetted against the night sky. She could see the outline of gargoyles and gothic arches. For a brief moment, she was sure she saw someone in the battlements above, by the light of the moon, then a bird flew overhead, and she realised it was that which she had seen.

'You daft thing,' she whispered to herself. She had walked through the grounds at all hours of the day, yet for the first time she had a sense of foreboding. She had never been called to see the mistress so late at night. She stood on the terrace, her hand ready to open the door when she heard a scraping sound from above, then before she could react, something, or someone, slammed into her, pushing her to the side and knocking all the air from her body. She hit the floor with a painful thud and a heavy weight on top of her. At the same time, something smashed to the ground where she had been standing, breaking into a dozen pieces.

'What the . . . ?' Polly looked up and realised that the heavy weight on top of her belonged to Anton, which was rather disconcerting as it felt a bit too nice. 'What on earth do you think you're doing?' Her heart pounded and her voice did not come out with the command she had hoped for.

'I think, my dear Boudicca, that I am saving you from the gargoyle which has just been pushed from the roof.'

4

'So you see, Greg, that it is very important that my grandmother knows that Polly was safe after that.' Lena looked up at him.

Greg, for his part, looked fascinated. 'I had heard this story,' he said, as if choosing his words carefully, 'But I thought that it had all been put down to an accident. I'm told the Priory was not very well maintained.'

'It was no accident, as my Nana found out later, after Polly and Miss Clara had left for Cariastan. May I see your grandmother now? Or if you know anything, perhaps you could tell me?'

'I know very little of this, only of a lady's maid who had been the victim of a possible assassination attempt.'

'You do know about it! Do you know what happened to her?'

36

'I'm afraid I can't tell you,' he said stiffly.

Lena looked at him, weighing up his words. He did not say that he did not know. Only that he could not tell her. There was a distinction. Or was she overthinking it? She had been on a night shift and was tired.

'Then may I speak with the Countess?'

'I will take you to her. Tell me, do you have a photograph of this Polly?'

'No. I'm sorry. Servants did not tend to be featured in photographs back then. From what I hear of the Harringtons, they would not have dreamed of putting their staff in the spotlight anyway.'

'Pity. I would like to have seen what this warrior maid looked like. Come, I will take you to Grandmother.'

Greg led Lena from the room, and up the grand staircase. 'She does tire very easily nowadays,' he explained. 'So you will forgive her if she is not very talkative. She also worries for my grandfather. They have not been separated for fifty years, and now she doesn't know where he is.'

'I hope he is safe. And it heartens me to know that there is so much love between them. I know . . . I hope you don't mind me saying that it was a marriage of convenience.'

'Yes . . . I suppose it was. All I have ever known is the affection they share, and the love with which they raised my father and my aunt.'

'Are your parents and aunt safe?'

'Thank you, yes. They are in America and we hope to join them as soon as the war is over.'

'It hasn't even begun yet.'

'I know.'

'I'm sorry, Greg, that came out sounding callous. I didn't intend it to.'

'What you say is true. I stay in Europe as long as I can to help the cause.'

By the time they finished speaking, they had climbed another, narrower staircase and made their way to a private suite of rooms on the second floor. Greg showed Lena into a pretty sitting room that overlooked the mall. It was filled with the aroma and vivid colours of fresh flowers. 'If you wait a moment, I will see if Grandmother can speak to you.'

Lena stood looking out over the mall while she waited. She could hear the low murmur of voices coming from the next room. One was unmistakably Greg's. The other belonged to a woman. Suddenly feeling warm, Lena opened the window, and heard words floating on the air from the window next door.

'Do you think she suspects anything?'

'No, I don't think she does, Grandmama.'

'Then I will see her.'

'Can it matter after all these years?'

'You're a good boy, Gregori, but I learned never to trust anyone. Take me to her.'

Lena shut the window with a louder bang than she intended, and moved away from the window to look at a painting. It was a lacklustre affair of the sea and a ship called the *Caria*, but she gazed at it as if it were the Mona Lisa.

When the bedroom door opened,

Lena turned and fixed a smile on her face. She had expected the Countess to be dressed like a dowager, in a flowing gown from another age, like Queen Mary. The woman who came in was wearing a navy Coco Chanel suit, with her silver hair expertly styled in a chignon. She was still very beautiful, and despite her age, had bright, intelligent eyes.

'Countess,' Lena said, curtseying.

'Oh, please, we don't stand on ceremony here,' the Countess said. 'Gregori will tell you that I hate all that bowing and scraping. So, you are . . . ?' She gestured to the sofa, were Lena sat down. The Countess sat on one of the chairs, her back ramrod straight.

'Lena Turner. My grandmother was Bessie Cooper. The cook at Derwent Priory.'

'She married Mr Turner, the butler?' The Countess clapped her hands together and laughed. It was a lovely musical sound.

'Yes, that's right. He was my grandfather. Sadly, we lost him to the Spanish flu.'

'Oh, poor Turner. I was always terrified of him as a child, but I also always suspected that he and Bessie — Mrs Cooper — were secretly in love. They would argue all the day long, but whenever Mr Harrington picked on Bessie, Mr Turner stuck up for her, and he would not hear a word said against her. So, they married . . . ?' The Countess's eyes became misty. 'How wonderful.'

'Are you alright, Grandmama?' Greg asked. 'If this is too much for you . . .'

'No, Gregori, I'm fine. I really am. It's just hearing those names, after all these years. So many memories of my life at the Priory. Some good. Some bad. But always these people were there, protecting me.'

'Countess,' said Lena, strangely moved by the Countess's reaction, despite her doubts about what she had overheard, 'I am here to ask you about Polly Smith. I believe she was your ladies' maid at the time.'

'Polly . . . I have not heard that name in such a long time.'

41

'My nana says you were friends, if that is not too presumptuous.'

'We were very good friends. We more or less grew up together. She was a couple of years older than me, but we had both had unhappy lives. I know she would have died for me.'

'That is what I am afraid of, Countess. My nana has not heard from her since a few months after she left with you for Cariastan. Do you know what happened to her?'

'Polly did not leave for Cariastan with the wedding party.'

'What? But she did. She was your maid. It was all planned.'

'I am aware of what was planned, child. But that is not what happened.'

'I am sorry, Countess, I didn't mean to be rude to you. My grandmother has always said that Polly left with you to go to Cariastan. Are you now telling me that's not the case?'

'That is exactly what I am telling you. Polly was due to leave with me the next morning, but she sent a note saying that she had decided to stay with the people she loved, and who had raised her. She said she had decided to stay with your grandmother. It transpired that Mrs Harrington had dismissed her and made her write the note.'

'But she left the Priory. She left and never returned. She wrote to my grandmother from Cariastan saying that she was with you. Are you saying that's not true?'

'I think the interrogation has gone far enough,' Greg said, putting his hand on his grandmother's shoulder. 'Doctor Turner, I understand your concerns for your grandmother's friend, but to speak to my grandmother in this way . . . '

'Please, Gregori,' the Countess said, patting his hand. 'It is alright. You are a doctor, child?'

'Yes.' Lena's face burned red hot. She was as upset about Greg's disapproval as she was about what she had learned. 'Yes, I am.'

'Your grandmother must be so proud of you.'

'She is. She knows how hard I have had to fight to get to where I want to be in a man's world. If not for help from a private benefactor when I wanted to go to Oxford, I would not be where I am now. And that's another reason I wanted to see you. I thought it might be Polly helping, and that she had asked you for help for me. That she had somehow been keeping an eye on us from afar. It's a romantic notion, I agree, but if I could go back and tell my grandmother that, she would know Polly was still with us in some way.'

'No one has asked for my help in such matters.'

Again, Lena was struck by the order of the words. It was not a denial, nor was it an admittance. 'Are you saying that you never saw Polly Smith again?'

'No, child. That is not what I am saying. I only said that Polly did not leave for Cariastan with the wedding party.'

5

Polly's heart was still pounding when she went into the garden room to see Mrs Harrington. The mistress seemed to have noticed nothing amiss, and stood among the plants, with her hands clasped together.

'What kept you?' she said, before waving her hand, dismissively. 'Never mind. You're here now.'

'Why did you want to see me?' Polly asked, adding, 'Ma'am' for good measure.

'I realise that you are attached to my niece, and she to you. You might believe that my husband and I are unaware of your sway over her young mind, but it is something that has given us concern for some time now. With that in mind, we have decided that you will not be travelling with her to Cariastan.'

'Are you dismissing me?' Polly asked, her heart giving an extra thump that almost took her breath away.

'No ...You may keep your post, for now. But you will no longer be Miss Clara's maid. You shall return to kitchen duties with Mrs Cooper.'

'But who will look after Miss Clara? Not Daisy? I know I've been training her, but she's not ready yet.' Polly felt a pang of jealousy. She loved Daisy as she loved all her workmates, but if she took Polly's place at Clara's side, it would be too much.

'Thank you. If I require your advice on staffing, I shall ask for it. No, Daisy will not be leaving us either. Mrs Lovett has agreed to take care of Miss Clara's needs until they reach Cariastan, then they will employ a local girl. I am sure they have ladies' maids abroad too.'

'She won't leave without me. I know she won't.'

'Yes, I am aware that you think you have this special friendship, but you are a servant and she is a high-born heiress.

You are not friends, nor can you ever be. When she is married and has children, she will have more to occupy her time than her silly dreams of equality among the heaving masses. Dreams that you encourage.'

'I hope that I do encourage them,' Polly retorted.

'Careful,' Mrs Harrington snapped. 'I could still change my mind and dismiss you.'

'She won't leave without me,' Polly repeated.

'Yes, she will and I will tell you why. You are going to write her a note saying that you have decided to stay with the people that you love, in the country that you love. If you do not, then the people that you claim to love — Mrs Cooper, Mrs Jenkins, Mr Turner, and everyone else in that happy band of lazy, over-eating, port drinking, creatures downstairs — might just find themselves without employment. Lord knows there are plenty of others who would simply jump at the chance to work here.'

Polly knew that much was not true. The owners of Derwent Priory were not known for their magnanimity towards staff. Nevertheless, it was a risk she could not take. Not with her friends' lives. But Clara was her friend too. How could she let her down?

'I have the notepaper ready in the study. You will come with me now and write it. Then you will go to your room, without saying one word to my niece. Any attempt to alert her to what you intend to do between now and her leaving will result in the measures I have outlined.'

'She will want to know why I am not going.' Polly's voice was barely above a whisper.

'Which is why she will have the note. Mrs Lovett will take care of dressing her in the morning.'

'Why can't I even say goodbye?'

'Who do you think you are?' Mrs Harrington's eyes flashed, angrily. 'You are a maid. A mere servant. It is not for you to say your goodbyes or hellos to people above your station. It is for you to obey your employer and keep your job. I knew I should never have had you here, the daughter of an actress. You were always going to be troublesome. He insisted. I think he does it on purpose to taunt me. He certainly does not do it out of any fondness for you.'

'Who do you mean?' Polly had heard the rumours about John Harrington and her mother, whilst in the orphanage, so none of this was a shock to her. This was the closest she had ever come to having it confirmed.

'Never you mind,' Mrs Harrington said. 'Just do as you're told.'

Polly had no choice but to follow her mistress to the study and write the letter that she dictated to her. She felt sure that Clara would know she had not written it, because the words were too formal, too stiff.

'You may end by wishing her well in her married life,' Mrs Harrington said. Once Polly had done that, the paper was snatched from her hand. 'Now, leave me.'

Polly took the back staircase to the servants' quarters at the top of the house. When she reached the last step, she turned around and sat down, putting her head in her hands. Until then, she had managed to hold off the tears, but now she let them go.

'What has happened? Has someone tried to hurt you again?' said a voice from behind her. It was Anton.

'Not physically, though I think my heart has just been ripped in two.'

He sat on the step next to her. 'What is it, Boudicca?'

'I'm really not Boudicca,' she said, woefully. 'I'm nothing but a coward. I wanted to stand up to her, but . . . sometimes you have to think of others, don't you? Not just yourself.'

'This is true, yes. Duty is very important. Tell me.' It was a command, albeit a gentle one. And it worked. Polly found herself telling him everything, only leaving out the part about John Harrington possibly being her father. She had never told Clara, even though she loved the idea of them being cousins. Making it public would only serve to remind people that she was illegitimate.

'I can't risk my friend's livelihoods,' she said. 'Yet, I'm afraid for her. Miss Clara, I mean. She's going to Cariastan with no allies. No friends. We are friends, no matter what the mistress says. Look, I know I haven't known you long, but you seem like a nice chap.'

'Thank you,' he said, his black eyes twinkling. 'I do not think I have ever been called a chap before.'

'You know what I mean. Will you keep an eye on her for me?'

'It is you I am most worried about. Someone tried to kill you tonight, then your mistress tells you that you cannot go to Cariastan. Do you not wonder why someone is trying so hard to stop you from leaving here with Miss Clara?'

'Yes . . . I mean . . . Oh God! I didn't think the two were linked. But why?'

'I do not know yet, but I agree that she needs a friend with her. Do you trust me, Boudicca? Even though I am just a

51

nice chap?'

'I think I do.'

'Then trust me when I say that I will make things right, if you are not afraid to be brave and maybe take some risks.'

'I'd do anything to keep her safe. Anything. But I can't risk hurting my other friends either.'

'You won't. I wish I had a friend like you.'

The feeling was more than mutual, and Polly went to bed feeling some hope for the morning.

However, when the morning came, and she woke up to begin her shift at five o'clock, it was to find that the wedding party had left in the early hours, taking Miss Clara with them. Whatever Anton had promised had not transpired and Polly was left behind at the Priory.

'I know you're unhappy,' Bessie Cooper said, pouring Polly a cup of tea at the kitchen table. She patted the girl's shoulder. 'But, I'm not sorry you didn't go. I would have missed you.'

'She's all alone, Mrs Cooper. At least

I have you. She has no one. He promised he would help me, but he hasn't. What if he's in on it all?'

'Who are we talking about?'

'Mr Anton. He said he would find a way for me to go, but he hasn't. They just left without me.'

'Young men often say things like that to girls, to impress them. I'm sure he meant it well.'

'I should have just gone. If I had the money, I would go. I'd follow them.'

'Now don't you go talking like that, Polly Smith. You can't go off running all over the world without a penny to your name. I was worried enough about white slavers when you were going to go with Miss Clara. I'd worry even more if you were all alone. We all would. You're a great favourite here, Polly.'

'The master and mistress wouldn't agree.'

'Well, luckily they don't run below stairs as much as they'd like to think they do.'

It had occurred to Polly that if she ran

away, her friends might be safe, because the Harringtons would just think that she had gone off in a huff to work elsewhere.

She spent rest of the day helping Bessie in the kitchen. Even though she was upset, she was a hard worker, and had the pots polished so well, Bessie could see her face in them. Then she cleared out all the cupboards, peeled potatoes and carrots, and made tea for the other staff, giving Bessie time to get on with her cooking.

By the time she went to bed, she was exhausted, but resigned to her fate. She had made a difficult decision and one she hoped Clara would understand. When she got to her room, she kicked off her shoes and sat on her bed, rubbing her aching feet.

What if she did run away? No one could be blamed then. If she did run away, how could she get to Clara? Even if she worked her passage, that could take weeks, or even months, to save the money needed. Her friend needed her now, not some vague time in the future.

That was when she saw the envelope on the bedside table, addressed to Boudicca. She opened it frantically, pulling out an open railway ticket for Dover and another, larger ticket for first class travel on the steamer *Caria*, with some money. There was a note saying, *Trust me.*

6

It was only when Polly left the Priory that she realised just how hard it was to leave her friends behind, especially Bessie Cooper.

It had been her home for ten years, and although it was not always easy to live there, because the upstairs family were so unhappy, she had been supported and loved. Sometimes bad employers resulted in bad staff, but with Bessie, Mrs Jenkins and Mr Turner running below stairs, somehow that did not happen. True they had a few who did not fit in and who left quickly, unable to deal with the atmosphere, but those who did stay did so out of love and respect for each other and out of for love of Miss Clara.

Polly was leaving all that behind and was not even able to say goodbye. She had packed a few of the dresses that Miss Clara had given her, sure that her own clothes would be no good in first class, and left in the early hours. She did not even leave Bessie a note, because she was afraid that it would cause problems with the master and mistress. Better for them all to think she had run away. She doubted it would occur to the Harringtons that she had the means of travelling to Cariastan on her own.

At the entrance gates, Polly took one look back at the Priory and said a silent prayer for her friends. It would have been very tempting to run back to the safety of their friendship, but they at least had each other. Clara had no one.

With a heavy heart, but fully determined to press on, Polly left the Priory grounds and set off into the unknown.

By the time she boarded the *Caria* at Dover, she was two days behind Clara's party, but it was still quicker than she could have managed on her own. It was only when she was in her ornate cabin, too afraid to join the other guests for fear of being outed as a common maid, that she began to wonder how Anton had been able to afford a first-class ticket.

Suddenly, Mrs Cooper's talk of white slavery was not so comical. Though whether white slavers would pay for a first-class ticket was another matter. Surely, she would be bound and gagged in the hold.

Her question was answered about ten minutes later. There was a knock on the door and a porter stood with a bouquet of flowers and a box of chocolates.

'Courtesy of Ambassador Lorenzo,' he said, putting the items on the table. He paused a moment and Polly realised he was waiting for a tip. She reached into her bag and took out a shilling, adding up in her head how much she might need for other things. She handed it to him.

He looked at it as if he had never been insulted in such a way before and left her with a not too silent 'Hmph.'

She sniffed at the flowers, which were a divine mixture of orchids and pink roses, then saw that there was a note. She opened it, expecting a kind message from the Ambassador. Instead, it said:

Dearest Polly,

I am so sorry. I had no idea what my aunt was planning. Thank goodness Anton told the Ambassador, who has agreed to help us. Please do not worry about Mrs Cooper and the others. I will continue to protect them as they have protected me over the years. You need not worry that you will be alone on the voyage. We have taken care of that too.

I will see you in Cariastan very soon.

Your friend,

Clara Harrington.

P.S. I think Anton likes you very much!

Polly burst out laughing, with joy and relief.

She kept to her room for most of the day, taking meals there. She knew she could not fit comfortably into the upper classes, even wearing one of Clara's finest gowns, and she was too honest a person to pretend.

Later that night, when the weather was calm and the moon was shining overhead, she went out onto the deck, to watch the sea for a while. The air was the clearest she had ever breathed. They had long since passed the coast of France and were heading south.

The moon reflected on the water, rippling and creating refracted light. She had a welcome feeling of calm. She knew that Clara was safe and that her friends back at the Priory were also cared for. She could begin to enjoy the trip.

'It is a lovely evening, is it not?' said a familiar voice beside her.

'Anton?' Polly turned to see him and for a brief moment had to stop herself from hugging him as the only familiar face. 'What are you doing here?'

'Miss Clara said that she would tell you that I would accompany you to Cariastan.'

'She didn't. She . . . Oh . . . she just said I would not be alone, but I thought she was speaking figuratively, like she was with me in spirit.'

'We agreed that it would not be safe for you to travel alone after what happened at the Priory, so I am here as your bodyguard.'

'I don't really need one,' she said,

despite the intense thrill running through her body. 'Whoever tried to hurt me, if indeed someone did, doesn't know where I am.'

'We can hope not,' said Anton. 'But we cannot be too careful.'

'But what about Clara? What if someone tries to hurt her?'

'No one will harm her when she is with the ambassador. They are travelling on the ship the *Dominique* with a dozen of Cariastan's finest soldiers, and their families, who are returning home after some time abroad. She is safer than you are at this moment.'

But probably not nearly as happy, Polly thought.

'Thank you for helping us,' she said, her voice thick with emotion. 'I will return the favour one day, if I can.'

'You owe me nothing. You and Miss Clara were badly used by the Harringtons, and I hate injustice of any kind, as does the ambassador.'

'I hope I get to meet him one day.'

'You will. He says he is looking forward to it. If you insist on doing me a favour, I have one request to make.'

'What is it?' Polly asked, cautiously.

'It is that you will not hide in your cabin for the trip. You will enjoy this voyage and everything it has to offer.'

'I'm not one of these people,' she said. 'I am grateful for everything, but I don't understand why I am in first class. I would have been just as happy in steerage.'

'You are safer here, believe me,' he said, mysteriously. 'Besides, Cariastan is not like your country. The class system is not so entrenched.'

'They still have counts, and dukes and princes — and a king!'

'Touché,' he smiled. 'Yes, this is true, but we are moving away from this, slowly but surely, with our new king and his queen. You will meet people on this boat who are self-made, who have worked their way up, and are grateful for their lot. True, some have become the snobs they hated, but that's unfortunate.'

'Are you in first class too?' she asked.

'I will not be too far away from you,' he said. 'If that is what worries you.'

'I wasn't worried,' she said, turning to look out over the sea.

This was all too perfect, wearing a pretty blue dress, standing there with a devastatingly handsome man, off on an adventure. She would wake up any moment and find herself in her attic room at the Priory, having to get up and start the day's chores.

'Good, because I was afraid you thought I planned to sell you into slavery. I gather it is Mrs Cooper's favourite nightmare.'

'She does worry so,' said Polly, missing the woman who had been a mother to her.

'When we get to Cariastan, you can write and let her know you are safe. But not until then. We can't risk the Harrington's finding out just yet.'

'I understand.'

'Now,' he asked. 'Would you like to go into the ballroom and dance?'

It was only in that moment that Polly

realised she wanted to dance with him
more than anything in the world.

7

At the same time that Polly was dancing with Anton, Clara's ship, the *Dominique*, had just passed the northern tip of Africa. She was a couple of days ahead of Polly, and despite the calm of the ocean, her head was still spinning at the speed at which she had been removed from her childhood home.

Like Polly, she had known difficult times at the Priory, but she had also known love and friendship from the people below stairs who cared for her more than her blood relatives ever had. She had been shaken awake by Mrs Lovett in the early hours. 'Come along, dear, we're leaving now.'

'Now?'

'Yes, we have had word of a threat against your life, so we're taking you to Cariastan as soon as possible.'

'I'm not packed.'

'We'll have your things sent on. Come

along now. Get dressed.'

'Can you call for Polly?'

'There's no need to wake the girl at this hour,' Mrs Lovett chided.

'But she's coming with us.'

'Your aunt says that she will follow on later.'

Clara dressed, perplexed by it all. She followed Mrs Lovett down to the hall where the ambassador waited, with his valet, Anton. 'You will catch up with us?' the ambassador was saying to Anton.

'Yes. You can be certain of it.'

'Are you sure this is the right way?'

'Yes. I am certain.'

They stopped speaking when they saw Mrs Lovett and Clara approaching them.

'Polly will be coming, won't she?' Clara asked them, her eyes wide with worry.

'I will make it my mission to get her to you,' Anton said, before the ambassador could speak.

'There, I said everything would be alright, didn't I?' said Mrs Lovett, casting a sharp glance at Anton. 'This footman will look after your friend.'

'Valet,' Anton corrected.

Mrs Lovett did not reply. 'Let us get this poor child out of the cold and into the coach,' she said to the ambassador. 'Otherwise, we will be delivering an icicle to the Count.'

Instead of going via train, as Clara had expected, they travelled by coach through the night until morning, and then they stopped at an Inn on the road to Dover. Mrs Lovett never left Clara's side for a moment, until Clara could stand it no more and went to her room to rest. At least there she could be alone.

She had rested for no more than a few minutes when there was a knock at the door. She opened it to find the ambassador.

'Excuse me, Miss Harrington for my impertinence, but I must speak to you in private, and it must be quickly. I have arranged for Mrs Lovett to be kept talking by a nun of my acquaintance, who is travelling with us to Cariastan, but I do not think she can hold her for long.

I must make you aware of some of the things that have been happening without your knowledge. May I enter?'

Clara stood aside to let him in, not doubting his sincerity. That was when she learned what had happened to Polly the night before, and how her aunt had blackmailed Polly into staying behind.

'Is Polly hurt?' Clara asked, horrified.

'No, I am assured that although she was winded by Anton pushing her out of the way, she has no bruises. She is, of course, very concerned about you, as we all are. We have reason to believe that the attempt on her life was really an attempt to stop her from travelling with you. There is talk among our best people of some plot against you, and I gather she is your fiercest champion. A warrior, Anton calls her. He is going to bring her to you. He will follow at a distance to begin with, then make his presence known when they are far from England. But she needs to be able to trust him. Will you write a note to her, that we can pass on, and let her know that we are on both your sides?'

'Of course, I will. But Mrs Lovett . . . '

'Appears to be an estimable woman, but in my line of business, one learns that it is best to operate on a 'need to know' basis. She does not need to know anything at the moment, as I am sure it would only alarm her more than my waking her in the early hours to fetch you.'

'Yes, of course, you are right. I will write your letter.' She took his old hands in hers. 'And thank you, Ambassador. Thank you for your help. Give my gratitude to Anton, when you contact him. I will thank him myself for saving Polly's life when I see him again. I am sure my future husband will want to show his gratitude for your kindness.'

'Given the circumstances, you would have no objections to your maid travelling first class on the steamer? It is unlikely anyone would bother her there.'

Clara laughed, and clapped her hands together. 'Oh, it will be wonderful for her! I only wish I could see her face when she gets on the boat.'

'You are a truly unique young woman.'

'Oh, I am rather ordinary and a bit dull. But I always take care of my friends, and if there is ever anything I can do for you, sir, then please ask.' She smiled. 'Anton must really like Polly.'

Instead of smiling, the ambassador became solemn. 'Yes. Yes, that is what concerns me.'

'Oh, but you mustn't worry. They're perfect for each other.'

He smiled kindly. 'I suppose they might be.'

'You're worried about losing your valet.'

'Yes, that is probably it. Good men like him are hard to find. Now, I must go before Mrs Lovett returns and thinks I am here for nefarious means. Although I should rather enjoy the scandal at my age, I would not wish it upon you. If you can try to give me the letter at supper . . .'

She agreed and showed him out of the door. Then she ran to her bed and lay back, laughing. 'Oh, Polly,' she giggled, and in a sing-song voice, she said, 'You have an admirer.'

Now, several days later, on the deck of a ship, looking at the same moon that Polly and Anton had enjoyed, Clara felt a pang of jealousy. Not about Polly or Anton personally, but about his obvious attraction for her friend. Would her new husband feel that way about her?

When she had decided her only escape would be through marriage, she had no thoughts of ever being in love. She never had been in love and was certain she never would be. The local young men paid court to her, but it was only because it was expected. None had made her heart flutter or even tempted her to share a kiss in the shrubbery. 'What if . . .' she thought to herself, 'I am devoid of love?'

Her parents had died when she was very little, just after brokering her marriage to the young Count, who was about seven years older than Clara. He was her cousin, but they had never met, yet their fate had been sealed from childhood in a legal and binding contract. Clara had resisted as long as she could, before she could bear it no longer at the Priory. Her aunt and uncle had only done their duty by her, and grudgingly at that, and had shown her no love. She was not sure if she was even capable of romantic love.

Yet, she loved her friend, Polly and she loved Mrs Cooper, Mr Turner (even though he scared her a little) and Mrs Jenkins. They had been her family. She and Polly had shared bedtime stories, learned how to dance at the same time — because Polly was the only possible partner — and she had helped Polly to learn reading and writing, while Polly had taught her the more menial labours, like how to light a fire, or change a bed. Clara had happily pitched in with the servants, because they were company for her.

Her aunt and uncle would have been horrified to learn how many times Clara followed the other maids around, changing beds, and mopping and dusting the upper rooms, darning stockings, ironing. It was mainly because she wanted to help Polly, so that they had more time to read or learn dancing. It also gave her an understanding of the hardships girls like Polly faced, with little hope of escaping a life of drudgery. She also understood that she could leave the drudgery behind whenever she wished, which was not a luxury afforded to Polly or Mrs Cooper.

It became harder to join in with household duties as she grew older and was expected to dine and take part in other pursuits with her aunt and uncle and their disapproving friends, but she remembered the back breaking work, and held the staff and their welfare in her heart. Because of that, she sympathised with the choice that Polly had been forced to make, about whether to stay or leave with her.

As well as writing to Polly, once on the boat, she had written a letter to her aunt and uncle. She was careful not to tell them what she knew, but she made it plain that her continued financial support depended very much on their continuing to employ the staff already at the Priory. She also wrote to the agency that supplied the staff and told them that she wanted to be informed immediately of any changes, tactfully reminding them of how much her trust fund had supported their services in the past and how she hoped to continue supporting them when she was managing a household of her own in Cariastan.

She finished the letters with a satisfied smile. Clara was kind, and sensitive, but as Polly had already recognised, she had a solid steel backbone when it came to protecting those deserving of her love and respect.

She wandered the deck of the ship, breathing in the cool air. Mrs Lovett had been struck by seasickness just out of Gibraltar, leaving Clara more time to be alone. Not that her companion had been unpleasant. She was a simple woman, with simple tastes, who stuck her nose up slightly at some of the richer foods on the menu, but she was not nearly as forbidding as Clara's aunt and uncle. For the first time, Clara began to get a sense of the freedom she had been missing all her life. She prayed the feeling would last.

She was walking near to the lifeboats, when a raspy voice called 'Look out!' and gave her a hard shove, knocking her under the stairway.

One of the lifeboats came crashing from its holdings, landing on the deck. At the same time, she thought she heard muffled steps on the deck above, which overhung where she stood.

'Oh, my goodness!' she cried. She looked into the darkness and saw a huddled shapeless form nearby. It moved nearer, until the light from the moon revealed a gentle face, full of wrinkles. Clara realised it was a nun.

'Those young men don't mind their work,' the nun said. 'I told the captain I thought these lifeboats could be tighter. Please forgive my impertinence in pushing you. I am Sister Marie Claire.'

'Clara Harrington,' she said, holding out her trembling hand. 'Thank you.'

'So, you are to be our new Countess. I was hoping to make your acquaintance.'

Several sailors came running from various directions, apologising for the disruption and working to put the lifeboat back on its mooring.

'Please, come into the salon and take a drink of something with me, Sister,' Clara said. 'It's a cold night.'

'I shouldn't, as our order practices temperance, but since you ask, I will share a double brandy with you — purely medicinal, of course.'

'Of course,' Clara smiled. 'I could do with something medicinal myself.' She put her hand to her chest, where her heart was still beating a rapid rhythm.

She led the sister into the salon and asked the waiter to bring two double brandies.

'Are you hungry?' Clara asked, noting the nun's rake thin fingers and sharp cheekbones. 'Unless your order practices abstinence with food too.'

'I could eat something,' the nun replied.

'When the boy returns, I will order sandwiches. I don't know what it is, but sailing somehow makes me ravenous.'

'It's the sea air,' Sister Marie Claire agreed. 'Apple pie for afters might be nice, also. With real custard if they have it at this time of night.'

'Oh yes,' Clara agreed. 'Erm . . . anything else?'

'Not at the moment. I will let you know.'

They drank their brandy, then ate in silence. Clara watched amazed as Sister Marie Claire polished off most of the sandwiches, wrapping the final two in a napkin and putting them into the folds of her voluminous habit. She then wolfed down the apple pie and custard.

'One of those cigarettes, lad,' the sister said to the waiter. 'The French ones. You don't mind?' she asked Clara, almost as an afterthought.

'Not at all,' Clara said. 'This order of yours must be very interesting. Are you Catholic?'

'Oh, good Lord no, child. We're Anglican, I suppose, but we make our own rules. Some of our members are married and live outside of the convent, but we all devote our lives to God's work. When I was a child,' she said, by way of explanation, as she smoked the strong-smelling cigarette. 'I was raised in a dreadful orphanage. We were starved and beaten, all in the name of God. I have never recovered from it, not really. I'm always hungry, yet always thin. I am always angry with God for the pain I suffered, yet I always love Him, because He is the only father I have ever known. I try to carry on His work. I'm but a poor sinner, and only try to do my best for Him. I fear I fail more than I succeed.'

'You probably saved my life tonight. I consider that a success.'

'Will it be enough? I don't know and I try not to think about it. I live in the now, except for times when I become melancholy and my mind must go back to those dark times. I make up for it by trying to ensure no child ever suffers as I did. My sisters and I travel the world raising funds for the orphanage at our convent in Cariastan. It was once a dark and horrible place. Now we fill it with light and laughter, and we teach the children that you can love God and love living at the same time. Not every transgression will result in eternal damnation. Not every mouthful of food has to be treated as a gift from God, to be prayed over and blessed, when for most people it is a basic human right to eat three meals a day. We do not beat them. We do not make them feel smaller than already they are. Do you understand what I mean by that?'

'Yes, yes, I do actually,' Clara said, her heart filled with emotions she could not name. 'I would like to donate, if I may. My dearest friend was brought up in such an orphanage. I would like to thank you in her name for what you do.'

'I knew the moment I saw you that you would be good for me. For our cause. Bless you, child. Perhaps, when you are settled in Cariastan, you would like to come and visit us.'

'I would be honoured, Sister Marie Claire. Is there anything else you need, before I turn in for the night?'

'No, child. You have passed my test. You have been amused by me, but not horrified or mocking. Like Cinderella with the fairy godmother.'

Clara laughed and stood up. 'Well, you have also passed my test. Had I ever such a plan in motion. I would like to talk to you more about your work, as we travel to Cariastan. May I?'

'We shall meet again on deck tomorrow, but not too early. I need my beauty sleep. Or at least I keep calling it that in the hope that He hears. Goodnight, child.'

'Goodnight, Sister Marie Claire.'

Clara went back to her own cabin. She could hear Mrs Lovett snoring in the cabin next door. She was supposed to wake her to help with undressing, but Clara let her sleep on, enjoying the moment of solitude. It seemed that all her life she had been watched. By her aunt and uncle, and also by the staff to some extent. She understood the concerns of the latter, but balked at the intrusion of her aunt and uncle into her every waking moment.

As much as she loved Polly, she also looked forward to the moment that Polly left her at night, shutting the bedroom door and leaving her to her own thoughts. It was in those moments that Clara felt she could truly be herself. As a child her dreams, as with most young women, turned to handsome princes who would save her from the castle in which she lay sleeping. Then, as she began to understand social injustice, she began to dream of helping those in need.

She could smile indulgently at her early fantasies, where she was the lady bountiful, bringing food, comfort and joy to people in ragged clothes. They were a child's dreams, based on needing to be loved, rather than any real wish to help others. As she matured, and saw the hardships the staff at the Priory suffered, her dream of self-aggrandisement petered away to become a genuine and heartfelt wish to help.

She had started by sending anonymous donations to various charities for the poor. Only small amounts, because her aunt and uncle watched every penny she spent, but it was a start.

That night, when she fell asleep, she did not dream of her future husband. He was still a shadowy concept, who would remain unreal until they met. She dreamt of all the people she might help when she had the means and opportunity to do so. Sister Marie Claire might be able to point her in the right direction.

In the early hours, her eyes snapped open from a dream in which she was handing out food to a queue of starving children when a lifeboat came crashing down, crushing her and her dreams.

8

'You were also in danger?' Lena said to the Countess. 'Thank goodness you're still here to tell your story. It must have been terrifying.'

'It was,' said the Countess. 'But it was also a little bit exciting. We were naïve young women, who had not known much excitement at the Priory. I do not say we enjoyed that time when it happened, but when I look back, I can appreciate the adventures we had.'

'So, Polly was alright when you met up again?' Lena realised that for everything she had been told, she had still not had an answer to her original question. 'Did she marry Anton? Is that why she left you?'

'Patience, child. Unless you would rather not know the rest of the story.'

Lena had to admit that she was fascinated by the Countess's adventures. The

Countess related everything with the art of a true storyteller. Lena had become invested in the tale of these two young girls, who had been thrown into an adventure involving romance and mystery.

Greg had taken up a place by the window, leaning against the frame, staring out. She had been aware of him the whole time. Occasionally he had rolled his eyes and laughed, presumably because he had heard the story so many times before. But there was something else that she could not put her finger on; times when he had been watchful, seeming as if he wanted to stop his grandmother from saying too much.

'I would like to know more,' Lena said. 'I suppose I just want to know there is a happy ending before you go any further. Although, I suppose you are a testament to that, since you are here. You are alive, and from what I gather, you and your husband did come to love each other very much.'

'He is the love of my life,' the Countess said quietly. Her face filled with pain.

'Now, we are apart for the first time ever.'

'I'm so sorry,' said Lena. 'I didn't mean to cause you pain.'

'Perhaps this is all too much for you, Grandmama,' Greg said. 'I can see it's churning up some difficult memories.'

'It's only in remembering all the people we leave behind as we move forward in this world,' said the Countess. 'One gets busy and forgets. No, not forgets. Never forgets. But it is too easy to lose those we hold dear just by getting on with life, and failing to keep the connections. Mrs Cooper, Mr Turner, Mrs Jenkins . . . they were my childhood and I have let them down.'

'What about Polly?' Lena whispered, noticing she was not among those mentioned.

'I will tell you,' Greg cut in. 'Polly left her job just before the wedding, and was never heard from again.'

'Is that it?' Lena asked, aghast. 'Is that all?'

'That is right, is it not, Grandmama?'

'Yes, Polly gave up her job as a ladies

maid and moved on to other things,' the Countess said, clasping her hands together.

'But you were great friends,' Lena said, emphatically. 'From what you have said, you were like sisters. I could understand you not keeping in touch with the others. They didn't travel to Cariastan with you. But Polly did, because she was worried about you. Or did that not matter once you became a Countess? Did you realise that your aunt was right and that you would never be equals?'

'That is quite enough!' Greg snapped. 'Doctor Turner, I allowed you to see my grandmother because I thought she might enjoy hearing about her old friends at the Priory, but I will not have you insult her in this way, or blame her for choices made by others.'

The Countess held up her hand. 'Gregori, don't fret so. I am tougher than I look.'

Lena picked up her bag and stood up, not caring if it was protocol or not. 'I apologise, Countess. I shouldn't have said those things. I suppose I became too invested in the story you were telling, but not all stories have perfect endings. If you say that Polly left you and went elsewhere, then I must accept that. I have to go. I need to rest before my shift tonight. I apologise for taking up your time.'

'I'll show you to the door,' Greg said.

'Thank you.'

The Countess stood up and walked to Lena, taking her hands in hers. 'Tell your grandmother that when Polly left, she was alive and well and missing her friend, Bessie.'

'What happened between you two?' Lena asked, sensing there was far more to the story than she had been told.

The Countess smiled, but her face was etched with the sadness of regrets from long ago. 'What always comes between two women who are great friends — a man, of course.'

9

Lena took off her mask and stripped out of the scrubs she had been wearing. It was two in the morning, and she was already exhausted. She had not slept much after her meeting with Greg and the Countess.

She went into the staffroom and slumped down at the table, putting her head in her hands. Five minutes. That's all she needed. Five minutes. She wouldn't get it. Soon they would call her again and she would have to perform another emergency surgery, or set a broken limb, or extricate some child's head from a saucepan.

She had a feeling of having made a great fool of herself, and wished she could reverse time and hold back on her anger.

Until the previous day, Polly Smith had been a shadow to her. One of the many names her grandmother spoke about from the past. Her nana had spoken about Miss Clara too, but not to the same extent. It was Polly that Nana had asked to see when she became ill a few weeks prior to Lena asking for an audience with the Countess.

'I just need to know that she was alright,' Bessie said, from her sick bed in the cottage in Scarborough. She had been retired for about fifteen years, working at the hotel they had bought until she was seventy. She lived in a cottage in the gardens, catered for by the staff who adored her. 'So, I can know I did right by her. She had no one else. Only Miss Clara.'

Lena had no real connection to the past, apart from her love for her grandmother, who had all but raised her while her parents worked long hours at the hospital. Her father had been a porter and her mother a nurse. The whole family had instilled Lena with the work ethic that had got her into medical school. She knew that she was named after Polly, who had been christened Paulina, but even that meant nothing to her. No more than her middle name being Mary, after her long dead great-grandmother on her mother's side.

Speaking to the Countess had changed that. Polly and Clara had been brought alive for her. She saw them as young women facing a dangerous world. She knew the ending to Clara's story: a happy marriage to a man she adored, and a handsome grandson. But Polly's ending still lay shrouded in darkness. Had she married Anton, the dashing valet? Was that why she suddenly left the friend she had fought so hard to protect? Perhaps the Countess resented her for it.

None of it made sense. The Countess had said it was a man, but that did not ring true either. The Countess was clearly smitten with her husband. If only Lena had not put her foot in it by accusing her of not caring for her friend.

'You're an idiot,' she murmured.

'I wouldn't have called you an idiot,' said a voice from the door.

Lena's head snapped up and she saw

Greg standing there, watching her.

'Oh, hello,' she said. 'Is your grandmother alright? I hope I didn't upset her too much.'

'She was quite amused. She says you have Bessie's temperament. She likes you.'

'I like her too. And I am sorry. What are you doing here? Surely you didn't come down here in the early hours to berate me for my behaviour.'

'No, actually I was looking for Doctor Kent. I was supposed to meet him an hour ago and he didn't turn up.'

'Mike? Mike Kent?'

'Yes. Is he working late?'

Lena stood up. 'No, no he isn't. In fact, I just left him in recovery.'

'Recovery?'

'Yes, sorry. Mike's appendix burst just over an hour ago. I've had to perform an emergency surgery. That's why he didn't meet you. He kept arguing he had somewhere else to be, but he would have died if we hadn't operated immediately.'

'Of course. Is he alright now?'

'The operation went well. You'll be able to see him in a little while.'

'I'm afraid I can't stay,' Greg said. 'We were going somewhere . . .'

He ran his hand through his thick, dark curls, and Lena had a sudden urge to share the sensation.

'I need a doctor.'

'Is it your grandmother? Is she ill?'

'No. She is well. I have to fly to Cariastan tonight. We've had word of where my grandfather is. But there are others with him, including some children who are sick. I have to get them out of the country before the war begins.' He sighed. 'Sorry to have bothered you. I'll make other arrangements.'

'When do you leave?' Lena asked.

'I have to go soon, so I can fly by night. I have an hour at most to get in the air.'

She knew what she was about to say was mad, but she could not just let him walk away. He looked lost and in need of a friend.

'Let me help, please. I can get someone to cover my shift.'

'You would do that?'

'Yes, of course. If it will help. I also owe it to you after my behaviour today.'

'I don't think being a little bit rude to someone warrants risking your life to save four more.'

'Let me help anyway,' Lena insisted. 'Because it's the right thing to do. Besides, I want to meet this grandfather of yours.'

Greg smiled. 'You'll get nothing out of him. He is as stoic as they come. Especially where my grandmother is concerned.'

'What's his name?'

'Gregori. I was named after him.'

That killed off one theory that had been brewing in Lena's head.

'Can you tell me more of the story, as we travel? Even if you can't tell me what happened to Polly after she left your grandmother's employment, I'd like to know more about what happened to them when they got to Cariastan. Did they find out who was trying to kill them?'

He laughed. 'I can't tell it as well as my grandmother does, but I'll do my best. I've heard it enough times. A story for a brave deed. It's almost as if they have been coaching me for this moment with you.'

'It's serendipity,' Lena said, her eyes fixed on his. 'You finding me instead of Mike.'

'You are much prettier. I feel a bit like Scheherazade. Are you ready for the first of our thousand and one nights?'

'I think, like you,' said Lena, 'I have been coached for this all my life.'

10

1890

'You are treading on my toes,' Anton said. The band played a waltz, but few were dancing that late in the evening. Just a few middle-aged married couples, while others watched from the side-lines.

'I can't help it,' said Polly. 'I always had to lead when I partnered Clara.'

'Perhaps you should remember that I am in charge,' he grinned.

'Perhaps I should stamp on your toes a bit harder, really show you who's boss.'

'I surrender. Shall we sit for a while and have a drink? It will give my toes time to recover.'

They went back to their table, and Anton ordered two cool drinks. The evening was sultry, as they reached the same area of the north African coast that Clara had passed a few days earlier.

Polly wore a simple white dress, with

a blue sash, but still the heat made her feel limp. Being close to Anton had not helped. Every night they had gone to the ballroom to dance, and Polly had her first taste of being a young lady able to enjoy a social life above stairs. She had even been asked to dance by other men, and she had agreed with a shyness that was unusual to her. They had not been quite as understanding when she insisted on leading or crushed their toes, but they had been far too British or well-mannered to say anything.

Anton was dressed in black evening attire that she could only assume he had borrowed from the Ambassador. Though she doubted the Ambassador looked quite as handsome in it.

'How did you come to be a valet?' she asked, as they looked out of the picture window at the night-time sea. Far in the distance there was a dark mass of land, with an occasional light flickering from the coast. 'You fit into this life so well. You could be an ambassador yourself.'

'It was a whim,' he said, guardedly.

'My mother was a governess, so I understand about being a servant.'

'Governesses in Britain aren't really servants. Not like I am. They often dine with the family.'

'This was the case with my mother. Then, when my father's first wife died, they became close and married. It caused a minor scandal, but they were too happy and too in love to care.'

'So, you have half-brothers and sisters?'

'I had a half-brother, but he died. Do you have brothers and sisters?'

'No, just me. I was left at the orphanage door when I was a baby. No one knows where I came from. Like Oliver Twist.'

'You could be a great lady.'

'I doubt it very much.' She did not want to tell him about John Harrington. It seemed better that her parentage was in question. 'Common as muck, me.'

Anton shook his head. 'No, there is nothing common about you, Polly. Look at the past few days. You instinctively know how to behave in, shall we say, fine company. You speak intelligently and well, albeit with that slight trace of Derbyshire accent you have.'

'Doesn't stop me treading on people's toes.'

'I have danced with many a lady who has left my toes bruised and battered. Not all of them excel at the fine arts. Not all speak French, or play the harpsichord, or embroider to perfection. The difference between you and them is that they don't feel the need to prove anything, because they already have their place in society.'

'You've done a lot, for a governess's son. Dancing with high born ladies.'

'I was in the army for a while. They are always desperate for young men to partner the young ladies at various balls and functions. What about you? Have you truly never danced with anyone other than Miss Clara?'

'A couple of lads at a local barn dance, but that's a bit different to this. With barn dancing you never get close enough to tread on toes. You're basically in the next county, waving at each other across the border.'

'Did you fall in love with any of them?' The answer seemed to matter to him a lot, because he waited eagerly for her reply.

'I did a bit, with one of them. A strapping farmer's son, with rosy cheeks and ginger hair. He was more interested in another farmer's daughter, because she came with about fifty acres. My heart was broken for about twenty-four hours, but I got over it.'

'You heartless woman!' Anton laughed, but there was also something else in his eyes . . . relief. 'He did not deserve you anyway if land was more important.'

'But it is, you see. If you've never been without, you won't know. A lot of the farmers in our area live from hand to mouth. They're paying tithes to the church, or extortionate rents to a local landowner, and one ruined crop can make the difference between a good year or a bad one. I don't blame him for choosing with his head, rather than his heart.'

'What would you have chosen? Duty or love?'

Polly thought about it for a while. 'The romantic in me would like to say that money doesn't matter, and that love is everything. The child who went to bed hungry because the owners of the orphanage spent the donations on good food and drink for themselves, understands that sometimes you have to make decisions based on need. The people who say that money doesn't buy happiness have never known the misery of starvation, or what it feels like to stuff their shoes with newspapers because they can't afford a new pair or even to have the old ones mended. I don't judge anyone for taking the easy road, because the hard road leads to drudgery and misery and children left on the doorstep of orphanages. Thankfully, I won't have to make any such choice. I'm never leaving Miss Clara's employment.'

'Even if you fell in love and he asked

you to marry him? You wouldn't give up everything to be with the man you loved? Name, reputation, livelihood, friendship?'

They looked at each other across the table, as Polly became lost in the question he had asked. Again, her answer seemed important to him. 'Are you . . . are you suggesting I would ever betray Miss Clara? Because I won't, no matter what.'

Anton smiled, but there was a certain sadness in his dark eyes. 'No, of course you would not. Not for anything or anyone.'

'Why do you even ask such a thing?'

He shrugged, as if throwing off a great weight. 'I just enjoy these philosophical questions, don't you? My father could debate all through the night, about ethics.'

'This is not just about ethics,' she replied. 'It's about morality too, and to betray my best friend would be immoral.'

'She is your friend, isn't she?'

'Yes. Why do you ask? Are you going to

give me the lecture about how we can't possibly be friends, because she's a lady and I'm just a servant? I understand the difference between us, and I respect that she will always be above me in station. But that doesn't mean I don't think of her as my friend.'

'I would never preach such a thing. Son of a governess, remember?'

'Sorry. I get a bit defensive, I know. I do worry that when she's a Countess, she won't want to be my friend anymore. She'll have a husband to confide in then, and she'll probably meet other ladies. Her aunt and uncle made sure she saw very few people outside their circle. That's probably why we became so close. There was no one else of her age she could confide in.'

'She chose her friend well,' Anton said. He turned to the window and looked out.

Polly wondered what to make of his demeanour. He looked sad. What's more, he looked lonely.

'We'll see each other from time to time, won't we?' she said. 'When you visit with the ambassador? There's nothing to stop me and you being friends.'

He turned back and looked at her for a long time. 'Yes, we can be friends,' he said, with a wan smile.

'Look at you, all gloomy. We've got a couple more days yet to dance and enjoy being in first class,' Polly said with forced cheerfulness.

He stood up, suddenly. 'I may be busy tomorrow. I have some things to do for the ambassador. If you need me, I will be there. Shall I walk you back to your cabin?'

Polly nodded, and followed him out of the ballroom, feeling that she had some-how said something very wrong.

★   ★   ★

In the early hours, Polly was awoken by a minor commotion outside her cabin. She put on her wrap and went to the door, opening it slightly.

There were a couple of the crew stand-ing on the deck, helping another man

103

over the railings. He spoke to them in a foreign language, but even Polly could make out he was giving them his thanks. Then, his head turned towards her and their eyes locked for a moment. His face was not as friendly when he looked at her.

Polly shut her door, as a shiver ran down her spine. She turned the lock sharply and stepped back, sure for a moment he would try to get in.

She heard the men walking past her cabin, the noise of their friendly chatter disappearing into the distance, but she still sat on the edge of her bed for half an hour before she felt secure enough to go back to sleep.

Even then, she slept badly.

The face the stranger had turned to her — if looks could kill . . .

11

1939

It was the early hours, and dawn was breaking in the east, before Lena started to question her rash decision to travel with Greg to Cariastan. They had driven to an airfield just outside London, where he picked up a small passenger plane, and had been flying east for a couple of hours.

She was in a plane with a man she barely knew, off on some adventure. Her Nana's frequent warnings about the slave trade came back to haunt her. Bessie, who had only ever travelled from Derbyshire to the North Yorkshire Coast had spent her whole life convinced that men were waiting to carry her or her loved ones off to slavery.

'We'll have to be careful,' he told her, through the headset. She sat next to him in the cockpit. Even with the headsets, it was hard to hear over the roar of the engine. 'We need to keep out of the sight of German forces. When we left, they had already taken northern Cariastan. Our last news was that they were moving south'

'How did your grandfather get left behind?'

'My grandmother and I were visiting an orphanage in the north when the Germans got over the border. I managed to get her out, but our route home was blocked. We had to leave by sea, so our only option was to make it to England. I would have stayed to fight, but I had to make sure she was safe. My grandfather, who had been unwell, was convalescing at the convent. Normally they go everywhere together. I pray he's alright. It's hit her hard, leaving him.'

'I'm sure he will be,' Lena said. 'He'll be thinking as much of her as she is of him.'

Greg's eyes gleamed, but she did not know if he was smiling or feeling sad. 'You already understand the depth of their love,' he said.

'If it was enough to break up a friend-ship . . . '

It was obvious that Greg laughed then. 'No, you're not doing that. You're not jumping ahead in the story and guessing the ending. It really matters to you, what happened to Polly Smith, doesn't it?'

'My nana always told me there were people in and out of your life all the time,' Lena explained. 'Some you barely noticed, because they were there for such a short time. Like all the footmen and housemaids who came and went from Derwent Priory. Others, she said, stayed with you, like an echo through time. She told me Polly was one of those echoes. She would say she could still hear her laughter, and see her dancing around the kitchen. She remembered her kindness and her courage. It's just sad that Polly's story ends so suddenly when your grandmother married. The more I can tell Nana, the better. And about your grandmother too. Clara was another echo through time. Nana loved them both.'

'We're reaching our destination. I will tell you more on the way, if we get a chance to talk.'

They landed in a small airfield. It was near the coast, at the very southernmost tip of the country. They got out of the plane, and made their way to a hanger, where several very attractive young men and women in plain working clothes were waiting, all armed with rifles. They stood to attention when they saw Greg. He saluted them back, then they all hugged, like old friends.

'Lena, let me introduce you to the resistance,' Greg said. 'God willing, once my family are safe, I will return to join them. My friends, this is Doctor Paulina Turner, who has bravely joined our cause for a short time.'

'Is everyone in Cariastan beautiful?' she asked.

'This lot? Beautiful? I think you must have dust in your eyes from the propellers.'

Stardust more like, Lena thought.

Especially where Greg was concerned. His demeanour had changed when they landed. This was so clearly his home. Even his clothes were more relaxed. He had changed into grey flannel trousers, and a chunky sweater.

'Have you checked on them, Ivan?' Greg asked one of the young men.

'Yes, Gregori, they are still at the convent near White Peak. We'll get you there, but we'll have to take the back streets. We've heard that the Germans have collaborators in the area. People sympathetic to the Nazi cause.'

'In Cariastan?' Greg shook his head. 'I can hardly believe it. What about the King and Queen?'

'You know King Henri and Queen Caroline,' said Ivan. 'They have said they will leave when everyone else has been evacuated.'

'How is that coming along?'

'Slowly.'

'I'll be back in a day or two to take more people,' Greg promised. 'And the *Caria* and the *Dominique* are returning for more passengers. They'll be here in a day or two.'

'Good,' said Ivan. 'Now hurry, both of you, we need to get going. We have a car waiting. We er . . . borrowed your grandfather's Austin Morris from his garage.'

Greg laughed. 'I'm sure he won't mind.'

'We'll follow you up to the convent, then form an escort coming back down.'

'Won't that draw more attention?' Lena asked. 'If there are spies watching? Won't they guess it's someone important if there's an escort?'

'She has a point,' said Greg. 'Follow at a distance, but be ready.'

Greg took Lena to a black Austin Morris outside the airfield and they got in. His friends stayed in the hangar, waiting for them to get ahead.

They drove through the early morning streets. Lena marvelled at the whitewash buildings, very similar to Greek villas, and the many church steeples, minarets and synagogues. It was hard to believe, as proud housewives scrubbed front steps, and men jumped on buses taking them to work on the docks, that only a few miles away, the German forces were holding onto the north of the country.

'It's idyllic,' she said to Greg. 'Just beautiful. I can see why you love it so.'

'Cariastan means the land of the Heart,' he told her. 'And it is engraved on all our hearts. True, we have had our share of good and bad kings and queens, and occasional political strife. Despite everything, the people have always been the same. Warm, welcoming and proud of our multicultural heritage. My grandmother claimed she had Vikings in her family, but I think she was teasing.' He stopped, as if he had said too much.

'Because?'

'Because that's what she does. She has a wicked sense of humour.'

Lena could not get over the feeling that he was about to say something else, and had changed his mind.

As they drove further north, the scenery changed. The villas and cottages gave way to a cosmopolitan city, with high rise buildings and classically styled museums and libraries.

'This is Caria, our capital. The convent is on the hill up there.'

Lena followed Greg's glance to a lush green hill, overlooking the city and covered in orange groves. High above the convent was a white chalky peak that stretched out over a valley filled with vineyards.

It took another half an hour to drive up the winding, and sometimes precipitous, path and reach the convent gates.

'You said you'd tell me more of the story,' Lena reminded him, as they climbed the steep path, the old Morris Austin creaking and rocking as it hit every pothole and rock.

12

Polly spent most of the next morning on the boat alone. She walked the deck, not as certain of herself without Anton by her side. He might think she could fit in anywhere, but she knew she did not. She had only learned how to speak properly and behave like a lady from Clara. Inside, she was still the gauche little ragamuffin from the orphanage. She convinced herself that was all everyone else could see.

She wore a yellow dress, with puff sleeves, and carried a white parasol, strolling the deck and wishing Anton was there to keep her company. When she reached the bow of the ship, she sat down on a deckchair, and watched a family group playing quoits. There was a mother and father, who appeared to be in their late twenties, and two children — a boy and a girl, not much older than five or six. The children giggled and screeched as the metal rings flew every-where but at the pin they were supposed to loop.

Other passengers tutted and sighed, and made a point of loudly opening their newspapers as they sat in their deck chairs.

'Ignore them, Violet,' the husband said to the wife, who struggled to keep the children quiet. He was clearly talking about the dissenters and not the children. 'There's quieter places they can go than the games area if they want peace.'

At that moment, the little girl threw a quoit so high that the wind caught it, and it flew off to the side of the ship and over the barrier. The little girl followed it, putting her foot onto the barrier and lifting herself up, reaching over. She put her foot up on the top rung of the bar-rier, lifting herself even higher.

'Charity!' Violet screamed, and started running towards her.

Polly was nearer. She jumped up from her deckchair and covered the space in double quick time, just catching the child's leg, before her top-heavy little body started to duck down the other side of the railing.

'Woah, there!' Polly said, holding Charity by one leg, then catching the other quickly.

Charity giggled — it was all a game to her! Polly flipped her over and put her down safely on the deck, the right way up.

'Oh, thank God! Thank you, Miss,' said Violet.

'Yes, thank you,' said the man.

'You're welcome,' said Polly. 'I'm just glad she's safe.'

'I'm Edward Shirebrook and this is my wife, Violet. You can call us Eddie and Vi, we don't stand on ceremony, like some.' He looked around at the snooty people on the deck. 'This is Charity and that's our lad, Joshua. Will you come and take tea with us, lass . . . I mean, Miss?'

'You're from Derbyshire,' Polly said. 'So am I, from near Matlock. My name is Polly Smith. You don't have to call me miss.'

'Oh, then we'll have plenty to talk about,' said Violet. 'We're from Chesterfield.' She was holding onto her fidgety children for dear life. Edward seemed blissfully unaware that she was struggling. Childcare was very much seen as a woman's job.

They went into the morning room, where they ordered tea and cakes.

'Do you know, you're the first person that Violet has dared speak to,' Edward said. 'She's been too shy to go to the dances at night.'

'They all think we're common,' she said to Polly. 'And I suppose we are to them. But Edward is a businessman.'

'I'm on my way to Cariastan to see if we can open up some trade with them,' Edward said, proudly. 'We make gloves. Did you know that the glove makers of Chesterfield learned a lot of their trade from Napoleonic soldiers who were prisoners of war?'

'No, I didn't,' Polly said. As she spoke,

she stood up and extricated little Joshua from under a nearby table where he had crawled. She sat him on her knee, and fed him cake while they talked. Charity was curled up in her mother's arms, sucking her thumb.

'Yes, the French taught them some new ways of glove making, and it revolutionised it. They settled in quite well, though they were enemies. There's even a gravestone in the Crooked Spire, written in French, English and Latin for one of them. Anyway, my family have been making gloves for years. Show her your gloves, Vi.'

Violet held out her hands, to show a very lovely pair of white kid gloves, with mother of pearl buttons.

'I'm going to Cariastan,' Edward said, 'to see if we can tempt them into doing trade.'

'They're very beautiful,' Polly said. 'I can sew, but those stitches are tiny.'

'That's Vi's work,' Edward said, proudly. 'She designs them as well. Or she did, before she got so busy with the little ones.'

'I just don't have time now,' Violet said.

She was pretty with an ample figure but tiredness left her with dark rings under her eyes.

'If you don't mind me asking, have you thought of getting a nanny?'

'We're going to bring our own kids up,' Edward said, before Violet could respond. 'None of that palming them off onto someone else to take care of like rich people do. My mum and dad raised me, and Violet's widowed mum raised her.'

'A mother's help then,' Polly suggested.

It was none of her business, but her kind heart went out to Violet. Edward was not a bad man, but he was like most men of his generation. He loved his children, and obviously adored his wife, but it was clear that he thought the care of them fell to her.

'You'd still be bringing them up, but Violet would have a bit of help with it for a few hours a day. She does look very tired,' Polly added for good measure, hoping that Edward really was a good man.

'Ay, that's true, Polly, she does that. No energy for anything, have you, duck? Tell you what, love,' he said to his wife. 'We'll look into it when we get back home, and I'll see if there's anyone in Cariastan who can help you while I'm busy.'

'Thank you,' Violet mouthed to Polly, the moment Edward turned his head away to ask the waiter for more tea.

'Do you have any sample gloves with you?' Polly asked. 'I should like to buy a pair for my friend.'

'Buy them?' Edward said, eyes wide. 'You'll buy nowt lass. Not after saving our little one's life. We'll give you pair. You and your friend. Let me go and fetch some.'

He bustled out of the salon, leaving Violet and Polly alone.

'I didn't think anyone was ever going to speak to me,' Violet said. 'Eddie said, 'We'll go first class, make a holiday of it', and I dreaded it. I wasn't wrong either. All these people just look down on us.'

'Not all upper-class people are the same,' Polly said. 'I've found that if you think you belong, you will. Though it's been harder today . . .'

'Without that handsome young man I've seen you with?' Violet said, her cheeks dimpling. 'I have noticed you. You make such a lovely couple.'

'We're not a couple,' Polly said. 'We just work together, and even then only temporarily. When my friend marries, he'll go back with his master to wherever they live and I will stay with my friend.'

For the first time in her life, Polly did not want to admit she was Clara's servant. Not that Violet and Edward would care, but for some strange reason, she suddenly did. She had been given a taste of freedom. A chance to just be herself and not be at someone else's beck and call all times of the day and night. She could get out of bed when she wanted, eat when she wanted, with more choices of dishes than she had ever experienced, and go back to bed when she was ready. Part of her wished it could go on forever, but she knew that was not possible. It was just a holiday from real life, which would soon come crashing in. She thought of Violet, who may be tied down by her children, but who had the skill of designing gloves that had contributed to the success of her husband's business.

Never before had Polly wished for something different. She had thought she would follow Clara everywhere, and she was still very fond of her. That did not stop her longing for something different. Something that was all her own, and not about how she related to another person. It would never happen. She was a servant and always would be, and she could have much worse employers than Clara. She did not really want to leave her, but the chance of doing something in her life that was not all about Clara was also attractive.

Edward returned with two pairs of white kid gloves, both with mother-of-pearl fastenings.

'Oh, they're beautiful. Are you sure you can spare these?' Polly asked. 'You must let me pay you for them.'

'I'll not have it,' Edward said.

'No, really,' Violet agreed. 'Take them.'

'Very well, then let me do something else for you both. You say you haven't been to the dances? Let me look after the children tonight so that you can both attend and dance together. I'll hazard a guess that it's a long time since you did that.'

'It has been a long time,' Violet said, wistfully.

'It has that.' Edward looked at his wife, and nodded. 'Very well, we accept.'

Polly spent the rest of the day in their company, tactfully stepping in whenever she saw Violet struggling with the children, but trying not to impose. They had lunch together, then sat on deckchairs while the children played nearby. They parted after afternoon tea, with a promise to meet up later.

All the time she thought of Anton and wondered if he would make an appearance. She imagined having to tell him she could not go dancing, and wondered if he would be disappointed. She was the one to be disappointed, when the situation did not arise. By the time she went to the Shirebrook's cabin at seven o'clock, she had not seen or heard from him all day.

On her way to the Shirebrook's cabin, she saw a porter go into Anton's cabin with some food on a tray, and she peaked inside briefly to see Anton sitting at a table, writing something. Then the door closed, and he was gone.

There had been something about the porter that was familiar, but she told herself that all the ship's crew had become familiar. They had all been confined to one relatively small space for several days. Crew came and went, and though one did not take great notice of them, their faces were bound to become part of the landscape.

She found Violet and Eddie all dressed up, ready for their night out.

'The children are in the adjoining

cabin,' Violet told her. 'The outer door is locked and we have the key, so they can't run away. I hope you don't mind, Polly, but I told them you'd read them a bedtime story.'

'I would be delighted to.'

'They've been reading *Black Beauty*. Charity loves horses.'

'Me too,' Polly said. 'Now, go on, you two. Go and enjoy yourselves.'

'You order yourself anything you want from the kitchens, Polly, and tell them to charge it to our cabin,' Eddie said. 'Don't you go hungry.'

'I've eaten so much this week, I'm amazed the ship is still afloat,' Polly laughed.

'It's the sea air,' Violet said. 'I think I've put on weight, too.'

'More for me to love,' said Eddie, proudly.

They left, promising not to be late, and the cabin became quiet. Polly went into the next room to see the two children sitting up in their own beds, looking at the book, their brows furrowed.

'Polly!' Charity called, jumping off the bed and running to her. Joshua followed, but not quite as confidently as his sister.

'Polly,' he echoed.

'I hear you're reading *Black Beauty*.'

'Just the pictures,' said Charity. 'I don't know words yet.'

'Then sit on the beds and I will read it to you. Which chapter did you get to?'

They insisted she start from chapter one, so that's what she did. She sat on a chair between the beds, and read to them for about an hour, only stopping briefly to take a drink of water. Every time she tried to stop reading, Charity would push the book back at her saying, 'Not sleepy.'

Finally, they both dozed off, which Polly thought was a pity as she was enjoying the story enormously herself.

She took the book into the next room and sat down on a love seat near to the porthole, losing herself in the story of the eponymous *Black Beauty*. Although she had learned a lot of the upper-class arts from Clara, riding had not been one of them. She read the book, flitting between the desire to ride a horse across a lush green field, and another desire to set every work horse in England free.

At the end of every chapter, she popped in to check on the children, to find them sleeping angelically.

At some point, she dozed off, and was awoken by Violet and Eddie returning, sometime late into the evening.

'Oh, I am sorry,' she said. 'I meant to stay awake.'

'You're lucky to get some sleep with that pair,' Eddie said. 'They'll have their mother up at six o'clock.'

'Or you could occupy them while she rests,' Polly said lightly.

Eddie seemed taken aback and for a moment, Polly thought she had overstepped the mark. 'Aye,' he said, laughing. 'I'll do that. I'll be mother, eh, Violet?'

'I'd like to see you try,' Violet giggled. She had returned looking years younger. 'Men have no idea where children are concerned.'

'I'll take that as a challenge,' Eddie said. 'You see if I don't.'

'Just read *Black Beauty* to them,' Polly said. 'They love it. I'd best be going.'

'Eddie, walk Polly back to her cabin. She doesn't want to be alone this time of night.'

'It's only on the ship,' said Polly.

'No,' said Eddie. 'Vi is right. I'll walk you back.'

If Polly were honest, she felt a bit awkward being alone with Edward but he turned out to be the perfect gentleman. All he could talk about was how much Violet had enjoyed herself. 'It was like courting again,' he said. 'I haven't seen her as happy in ages.'

'I'm so glad,' said Polly. 'If you want to do it again before the voyage ends, just ask me.'

'Aye, I might do that, lass,' he agreed.

They rounded the corner to Polly's cabin, and saw a shrouded figure huddled over near to her door. Whoever it was, knocked weakly.

'Hello?' she said. 'Can I help you?'

The figure turned around, revealing a man wrapped in a ship's blanket. His pallor was like that of a ghost, grey and sickly, and it took a moment, as he stepped into the light, for Polly to realise who it was.

'Help me, Polly,' Anton said, before falling into her arms in a dead faint.

13

As Anton was falling into Polly's arms, Clara was finally arriving in Cariastan. The ocean shone like a million sapphires in the sunlight as she disembarked with the Ambassador and Mrs Lovett.

There was a fine carriage waiting for them, pulled by black horses.

'I have had word that the Count is delayed in the south,' the Ambassador explained. 'He will join us in a couple of days. Now come, we have a long trip to Caria.'

Clara felt a pang of disappointment, but also a great feeling of relief. She could put off meeting her husband for a little while longer.

As they climbed into the carriage, aided by footmen in blue and gold livery, Clara saw Sister Marie Claire struggling down the gangplank with a large trunk. 'Can we help her?' she asked the Ambassador. 'She's my friend.'

If he was surprised, he was too much of a diplomat to show it. He must have known that Clara had spent a lot of time in the sister's company.

'Where are you going to, good sister?' he asked the nun.

'The Sacred Heart convent, up on the White Peak,' she replied.

'Then you can travel with us to my villa, and I will have the coach take you on to the convent. If that is acceptable?'

'That is very kind of you — and Miss Clara. Thank you.'

The footman lifted the nun's trunk onto the back of the carriage, and then helped her inside.

'Mrs Lovett, I don't think you have met Sister Marie Claire. She chaperoned me ably while you were unwell.'

'Then I thank you for your service,' Mrs Lovett said. 'It is a comfort to know that Miss Clara was in God's hands.'

'Are you well now, Mrs Lovett?' asked Sister Marie Claire.

'I am, thank you.'

'I thought so, because I saw you walking on deck yesterday.'

'It can't have been me,' said Mrs Lovett. 'I'm afraid I was in my bed till we docked this morning.'

'Must have been your doppelganger,' said the sister. 'Same taste in hats and everything.'

Clara listened quizzically. If Mrs Lovett was out on deck, why lie about it? Or was the sister teasing? In the preceding days, Clara had learned that she had a very strange sense of humour.

They drove on for a while, with no one speaking. Clara tried to take interest in her new home. It was true that Cariastan was beautiful. Houses and villas of white stone lined the highway, and lush green field covered the landscape. Far in the distance, she could see snow-capped hills, with an azure blue sky above. The air was crisp and fresh, despite the heat.

The road was a little uneven, cut as it was into rock, so the going was slow and laborious at times, shaking the carriage and Clara's nerves with it. She should have felt annoyed that her future husband was not there to meet her, yet it gave her breathing space and time to think about what she really wanted.

'Tell us about the convent,' Clara asked, to cover over the slightly uncomfortable atmosphere. 'And what is the White Peak?'

'It's a treacherous place,' the sister said. 'Beautiful, but deadly. 'So many people have lost their lives.'

'Not that many,' said the Ambassador. 'And not for about twenty years or more. People are more aware of it now, and take greater care. Only last year, after another near accident, government put up a barrier to stop people from going too near to the edge.'

'Did they?' asked Mrs Lovett, sharply. 'All I can say is that it took them long enough.'

'Yes,' said Sister Marie Claire, looking Mrs Lovett up and down. 'An elderly man from England was on business here, and he went to look at the Peak with some friends, who say they lost track of him. They found him hanging by his fingernails from the edge of the cliff. He swore someone had pushed him. Then, about twenty years ago, a young married couple had come to Cariastan, to visit relatives, and they were found dead on a ledge a hundred feet below. They say it was a suicide pact, but they had a child at home and everything to live for. The coroner ruled it an accident, so that they could be buried on sacred ground.'

'Can we stop the carriage?' asked Clara. 'Please, quickly. Stop!' She jumped out before the carriage had come to a full stop and leaned over, sure she would be sick.

'Miss Harrington,' the Ambassador said. He had followed her out. Mrs Lovett stayed in the carriage, with the sister. 'I apologise profusely, he said. 'Such talk is not fitting for young ladies.'

Clara straightened up. Her whole body shook. She was not the sort of young lady given to the vapours, but for the first time she thought she might pass out.

'I am being silly. I'm sure it's just a coincidence. I'm ready to move on now.'

'A coincidence?' asked the Ambassador.

'I was only little when it happened, but the story I have been told by my aunt and uncle is that my mother and father travelled to Cariastan to broker my marriage to the Count, and this is where they died. My aunt always told me that they had taken their own lives, but that people in high places had covered that up and ruled as an accident so as not to bring shame on the family.'

'My poor child,' the Ambassador said. 'I am so sorry for your loss.' Her voice fell below a whisper. 'With everything that's happened with the attempt on Polly's life and the lifeboat nearly landing on me, what if it was neither suicide or an accident? What if they were murdered?'

14

'Your poor grandmother,' Lena said. 'Did she ever find out the truth about her parents?'

'We're nearly at the convent,' Greg said. 'I may not be able to finish the story until this is all over, and I don't want to discuss it in front of my grandfather. It was a very difficult time for them.'

'Yes, of course.'

Lena understood they had more pressing concerns. All the way to the capital, she had been convinced they were being watched or followed. Or both. There was no solid proof. Just a niggly feeling in the back of one's neck that all eyes were on them. It might have been paranoia, but there was no doubt that people were watchful. Either because they were spying for the Germans, or they feared they were being spied upon.

The convent rose before them halfway up the mountain. It was constructed of yellow stone in the Byzantine style, with pillars supporting curved archways and high, narrow windows. It stood as a monument to craftsmanship and the ravages of time. Some of the stonework was damaged on one side, and several windows were boarded up, presumably because glass had been expensive at the time they were broken. Yet, it appeared solid, dependable and safe.

'It's said that it once belonged to a sheik,' Greg explained, 'But he left it to return to fight in a medieval war and never returned. The nuns pretty much moved in and took it over without asking, turning it into God's house. No one has ever dared challenge them for the rights to it.'

Peace emanated from its walls, and made it even harder to believe that the enemy was entrenched just a few miles away. She even wondered if there was anyone inside its walls. It was truly closed off from the world.

Greg stopped the car and they got out, walking up to a large oak door that had a small opening at head height. Greg pulled on the bell and they could hear it chiming within. It was taking so long that he was about to tug at the bell again, when the aperture opened and the top of a wimple appeared.

'Yes, my child, who is it?'

'It's Gregori de Luca. Is that Sister Dominique? The password is Victoria sponge,' he quipped.

'Gregori! God be praised.'

There was the sound of keys being turned and barriers being drawn back, then the door opened to reveal a nun with the most beautiful and placid face that Lena had ever seen. It was hard to tell her age, though Lena supposed that she must be in her later years.

'Come in, come in.' She beckoned them, and shut the doors behind them.

Greg hugged her warmly. 'Thank God you're still here,' he said. 'Lena, this is my father's godmother, Sister Dominique.'

'And who is this lovely young woman?'

the sister asked.

'She's the granddaughter of an old friend of my grandmother's,' Greg said. 'Her name is Doctor Lena Turner and her grandmother was Bessie Cooper, who used to be a cook at my grandmother's old place in England. You'll have heard the Countess talking about her, I'm sure.'

Sister Dominique gazed at Lena for a long time, as if memorising her face. 'Bessie Copper's granddaughter, here? Of course, I have heard of Bessie. The Countess talks of her all the time.' The sister swallowed hard, as if she was biting back some emotion.

Lena was about to ask a question but Greg put her hand on her arm, as if he knew what it was going to be. 'Where is my grandfather?' he asked. 'Is he well'

'He's as stubborn as he ever was,' said Sister Dominique. 'Keeps insisting on doing things when he should be resting. So yes, he's well. Come, I'll take you to him.'

She led them through the convent,

limping slightly. It was the only hint to her great age.

Lena had been right about the peace inside the convent. It was not a silent order, as every now and then, when they passed rooms, they would hear hushed voices. The peace came from the nuns, who seemed to float through the corridors. It helped that, despite the heat outside, the air inside was cool and refreshing. She imagined that might not be such a good thing in winter, but she was hot from the journey, having put on a sweater and slacks before she left England, so she welcomed it.

'I thought you said everyone had been evacuated,' Lena said to Greg.

'Everyone who wants to leave. The nuns won't give up the convent that easily.'

'And nor should we,' said Sister Dominique. 'We've seen off other invaders over the years.'

'You're coming with us, aren't you?' Greg asked. 'My grandmother has told me to bring you, even if you argue. I still

139

haven't decided yet which one of you I am more afraid of.'

'You know we're both pussycats, really, Gregori. Yes, I'll come, but only so that the children have a familiar face on the journey. Then I will return to my sisters. I'll argue about that with your grand-mother when we see each other again.'

'Did you know Sister Marie Claire?' Lena asked Sister Dominique, earning a sharp glance from Greg.

'Why, yes I did. She is long gone now, bless her soul. She was a true character. Not quite as holy as one would expect, yet kind and honest. I never could quite learn her love of French cigarettes.'

'We can talk of this another time,' Greg said. 'Where is grandfather?'

Sister Dominique led them to a room at the far corner of the abbey. It was at the end of a long row of similar rooms, which looked more like cells. Rectangular stone structures, with one narrow window, set too high to be able to look out. Most cells were empty with the doors ajar. They were only about ten feet

140

by six feet, with one truckle bed and a small dresser and bedside table. Despite the size, the beds looked comfortable and the rooms were spotlessly clean.

'We used to host retreats,' Sister Dominique said, as if noticing Lena's interest. 'The frazzled wives of businessmen used to come here, or the elderly, looking for some peace at the end of their days. Then we became an orphanage. Most of the children have been evacuated, or placed in loving homes, but Reuben had a fever and his sister, Rachel, refused to leave him. We have been trying to find a family who would take both children, but eight-year-olds are difficult to place on their own, let alone in twos. Everyone wants a baby, so they can shape it to their own way of life. Older children have already begun to develop their own personalities.' She paused outside a closed door. 'This is your grandfather's room.'

She knocked and a low voice within told them to enter.

Greg almost flew over the threshold.

'Grandpa!' he cried, and ran to hug the elderly man who stood at the side of the bed.

'Gregori!' The two men hugged for a long time, and Greg was saying something to his grandfather that Lena could not hear, but it had the tone of a warning. Feeling that she was intruding, she stepped back into the corridor, where Sister Dominique was also waiting.

'Have you known the family a long time?' she asked her.

'All my life,' Sister Dominique said.

'Did you know the Countess before she married?'

'I knew both of them before their marriage. The Count and I are related.'

'Did you ever know one of the Countess's ladies' maids, Polly Smith?'

'I knew of a girl called Polly, yes,' said the sister, her eyes watchful.

'I've been looking for her. But she seemed to just disappear. My grandmother would just like word of her. I don't suppose . . .'

'Is she cross-examining you, Sister

Dominique,' Greg said from behind them. 'She does that.'

'It is not cross examining to seek the truth, Gregori,' the sister chided. 'She has a good soul. I can feel it. Your grand-mother must be very proud of you, child,' she said to Lena.

'She is,' Lena said. 'I am proud of her too.'

'You must tell me all about her. I have heard about her, of course, but I would like to know what she has been doing since the Countess left her.'

'We'll have time for that later,' Greg said.

'Right now, we need to eat, then set out for the south. Are the children ready?'

'I will take you to meet them,' said Sister Dominique. 'Perhaps Doctor Turner could look them over.'

'Gregori,' the Count cut in. 'You have not introduced me to this charming young woman.'

Greg made the introductions. The Count, despite his great age, was a very handsome man, with a straight back and proud bearing. Yet, there was a twinkle in his eyes that softened his otherwise imposing countenance.

'So,' said the Count. 'You are Bessie's granddaughter? She was quite a formidable woman.'

'I had no idea you had met her,' Lena said.

'I am told by my wife that she was quite a formidable woman. But one with a big heart.'

'Yes,' said Lena. 'A huge heart.'

She knew better than to ask any more questions about Polly. It seemed that every time she mentioned the young maid, everyone became guarded. She did not want to spoil the rapport she had built up with Greg by pressing too much. She was surprised by how quickly his good opinion had come to matter to her.

'I'm very pleased to meet you, sir,' she said. 'Perhaps I could look at the children now?'

Greg and his grandfather elected to stay behind in the bedroom to make plans for their trip to the south. Lena followed Sister Dominique to a different part of the convent, where the cells gave way to larger rooms, holding four beds each.

'This is the orphanage,' the sister told her. 'Though there had been an orphanage at the convent for some time, this particular wing was founded by the Countess just after her marriage. She told us that the conditions in English orphanages were terrible, so we did our best to ensure this was a place of love and encouragement, with a loving God who understands that sometimes we make mistakes and the important thing is to learn from them. One doesn't learn anything from the end of a cane, other than to not get caught next time.'

'My nana told me that her friend, Polly, was half-starving when she was sent from the orphanage to work at Derwent Priory.'

'Yes, I have heard such things.'

The Sister led Lena into one of the rooms. One side was unused, but the other had childlike paintings on the walls and piles of books next to the beds. Two children, a boy and a girl with dark hair, sat huddled together, looking at one of the books. When they looked up, their faces were not identical, but it was obvious they were brother and sister.

'Reuben, Rachel, this is Doctor Turner. She's here to make sure you're well enough to travel.'

'Hello, children,' Lena smiled. She put her medicine bag on a bedside table. 'I hear that one of you has been poorly.'

'That was Reuben,' said Rachel, fixing large brown eyes on Lena. 'I'm never ill, but he gets a lot of fevers. Don't you, Reuben?'

Reuben nodded. 'But I can help you to escape,' he promised. His breath was wheezy. 'I'm not a coward.' He followed his words with a cough.

Lena smiled. 'It doesn't make you a coward to be ill,' she soothed. 'Some of the bravest people I know have serious health problems. It takes courage to face every day knowing you're going to be in pain. May I listen to your chest, Reuben?'

Reuben looked at his sister, who nodded. 'It will be OK Reuben. They have lady doctors now.'

'You speak very good English,' Lena said.

'Our mother was English,' Rachel said. 'She fell off the White Peak.'

'I . . . I'm sorry.' Lena was struck by the matter-of-fact way the child said it. As if it was something that happened every day.

'It's alright. We were only five then and we're eight now. We sort of remember her, but it's like watching a film in our heads. Sister Dominique sometimes takes us to the cinema. We saw *The Scarlet Pimpernel,* which we both liked, didn't we Reuben?'

'Are we going to escape dressed as French peasants?' Reuben asked.

Lena laughed, taking out a stethoscope. 'It would be fun, but I don't think that will be necessary. Come on, let's listen to that chest.'

147

Lena first gave Reuben a thorough examination, then Rachel. 'We're just going to talk outside,' she told them, gesturing for Sister Dominique to go into the corridor.

'That means we're going to die, doesn't it?' asked Rachel, as if she found the idea quite interesting.

'No.' Lena held both their hands, speaking emphatically. 'You're not going to die. Not with me as your doctor, alright?'

They both nodded, seemingly appeased. Lena took Sister Dominique into the hallway, shutting the door behind her.

'I'm afraid he has fluid on his lungs,' she said. 'It's possibly pneumonia.'

'Is he well enough to travel?' the sister asked. 'Because he can't stay here. Not with the Germans at the door. Their mother was a Jew. I've heard about the terrible things that happen to Jews in Germany.'

'We have to get them out, so he can get treatment in a hospital,' Lena said. 'It's the trip to England I'm worried about. We'll be at high altitude. We need oxygen, just in case. Do you have any?'

'No, but we could get some from the local hospital.'

'Good. I'll get Greg to take me.'

She went back into the room to assure the children that everything would be alright. As she opened the door, she heard a scuttling noise.

'People sometimes die from pneumonia, but Reuben won't because I won't let him,' Rachel said, proving she had been listening at the door.

'You'll make a good spy against the Nazis,' Lena laughed.

'Yes, I rather think I would.'

'You just need to learn to return to base quietly,' Lena teased. 'You ran back to your bed with all the subtlety of a baby elephant.'

Reuben giggled, which turned into a hacking cough. 'We're going to get some oxygen,' Lena told him. 'To help you to breathe easier when we're flying.'

'We're going on an aeroplane?' he

said, his eyes widening. 'We've never be on one, have we, Rachel?'

'No, we came with mama by boat. An aeroplane will be very exciting.'

'Wait here,' Sister Dominique told them, stroking each of their heads. 'We'll come for you when we're ready to leave. Make sure you eat all your food today, even if you don't feel like it. You're going to need your energy.'

'That's just an excuse to get us to eat Sister Theresa's rock-hard carrots,' Rachel sighed.

'They're very good for the eyesight,' Lena said. 'Important if you want to be a spy.'

'Oh yes ... Though I may just be a ballerina.'

'In that case, you need the iron for strong bones.'

'You have an answer for everything.'

'No, I've just heard every excuse,' Lena laughed.

'She's very clever,' Lena told the sister as they went back to the Count's room.

'Yes, which is why she needs to attend

a proper school. We do our best here, but we can't give them the breadth of education they need, such as the sciences and biology. We're not against the theory of evolution, like some Christian religions. We believe it has its place in God's great design. We just don't understand evolution as well as we need to,' the sister explained.

'For what it's worth, I think you're doing a fantastic job. They're wonderful children, even if Rachel has a bit of a fixation with death.'

'It's not surprising, considering what happened to their mother. She had come here to escape their father.'

'Was it an accident?' Lena asked. 'Because I've heard things about White Peak . . .'

'White Peak,' said Sister Dominique, with a sharp edge to her voice, as she walked on ahead. 'Is just a place. What evil or anguish people bring to it is their own. Not the place.'

'I'm sorry. I didn't mean to . . .'

The sister stopped. 'I apologise for

my anger. It's just that the children do listen to stories about it from the gardeners and workmen, then they become fixated, as Rachel is. It is not healthy to concentrate so much on a place that has stood for millions of years, yet perhaps only seen half a dozen deaths. Not that those deaths weren't tragic. They were. But it is important to keep perspective. Otherwise, one might find oneself drawn to the place, believing it has the answers to everything.'

'Of course.' Lena shivered, as if a chill had come over the convent. 'You're quite right.'

They reached the Count's bedroom, to find him with Greg and another man, who was dressed in work clothes.

'We have a problem,' Greg said, when he saw them. 'Vincenzo here tells us that we've been seen by the collaborators. We can't leave in my grandfather's car. We have to find another way to get back to the south. And we have to leave now, before they can pass on the information.'

15

The Count told them, 'There is a way around. If we can get to the coast, we can take a boat to your aeroplane. It will take longer, but we won't be as visible.'

'Very well,' said Greg. 'But first we need to get past the spies.'

'I can help,' said Vincenzo. 'I have a load of vegetables on my truck to take to the bazaar near to the docks. Sometimes the sisters accompany me to sell them on the stalls. Sister Dominique, do you have a habit for the young lady?'

'Yes, of course. I'll go and fetch one. What about the children?'

'No one is looking for children,' said Vincenzo. 'As far as I know. They can lie among the cargo with the Count and Mr de Luca. Sir,' he said to the Count. 'If you and your grandson can find working clothes, just in case you are spotted, that might help. And perhaps muddy your faces and arms a little.'

'We can do that,' said Greg.

'Greg,' Lena cut in, 'We have another problem. We need an oxygen canister for Reuben.' She explained about the little boy's health and the dangers of them reaching high altitudes when his breathing was already so laboured. 'We need to stop at a hospital.'

'That might not be safe,' said Vincenzo. 'It might be noticed if I stop in the city too long.'

'Then could you get one of your other people to fetch one and meet us at the plane, Greg?' she asked.

'Yes, I'll do that,' Greg agreed. 'Sister Dominique, may I use your telephone?'

'Of course, child.'

* * *

Lena was hotter than ever, wearing a thick habit and wimple over her existing clothes. The sun shone through the windscreen of the truck, causing tiny beads of sweat to prickle on her forehead. They had waited until late afternoon, so they

154

could leave the docks under cover of night, but the sun was still blistering hot.

'Do you think the children will be alright?' she asked Sister Dominique.

They were sitting with Vincenzo in the cab of his truck, three of them huddled together on one long bench seat. It made Lena feel claustrophobic, as well as overly hot. She opened a window, but it would only go so far before the mechanism got stuck, and there was very little breeze to speak of, even with the cab window open anyway.

'I am sure they are enjoying every minute of it,' the Sister replied.

Reuben and Rachel had viewed the whole situation as a big adventure, which made it easier to put them under a tarpaulin with the Count and Greg. Lena was concerned about how the heat and dust would affect Reuben's breathing, but she had to hope that the relatively short journey to the docks would not harm him too much.

Greg had managed to contact one of his friends, who was going to meet them at the airfield with the oxygen. She was surprised to see that both Greg and his grandfather were armed with rifles. She hated the idea of the weapons being around the children, even while understanding the reasons.

'I will take care of my brother,' Rachel insisted.

'I know you will, darling,' Lena said. 'You're both very brave. Reuben, if you feel you can't breathe, tell Greg or the Count, alright?'

'Yes, Miss,' Reuben replied.

'He can have my breath,' Rachel said. 'I've seen people do it on films.'

The child's touching care for her brother made Lena want to cry. How could no one want both these children in their lives?

She began to think about how she might help them when they were in England. She had married friends who couldn't have children. She would approach them and see if they were interested. Deep down a voice urged her to take care of them herself, but she pushed it away. She was in no position to bring up two children. Women tended to have to choose career over family, and she knew that any time out to take care of a child would impact on her chances for promotion. She had worked too long and hard to become a doctor to give it all up for the sake of a sentimental whim.

They travelled down the mountain, and back into the city. The truck lacked adequate suspension, so it hit every boulder and pothole with twice the force of the Count's car.

They had just reached the edge of the city when a shot rang out and the truck seemed to buckle and spin, before ending up facing the way it had been heading. Vincenzo put his foot down on the accelerator.

There was a loud banging on the back window of the cab. Lena turned to see Greg there, gesticulating. 'Faster!' he called.

'Faster,' she repeated to Vincenzo. Sister Dominique had turned grey.

'Oh, yes, I had not though of that!'

Vincenzo said, tetchily. 'Maybe he can find me a bigger engine while he is full of good ideas!'

'Are you alright?' Lena asked the Sister.

'Yes, yes, I've been in tighter situations than this. Go on, Vincenzo. Do as the man says.'

The next five minutes were a blur to Lena, as shots rang out, both towards them and from the back of the truck to some unknown destination above them; perhaps windows or towards rooftops where snipers hid. Vincenzo slipped in and out of side streets, as if trying to lose their tail. Lena prayed for the children's safety. She wanted to ask if they were safe, but when she turned, she could see that Greg and the Count had more pressing concerns.

Another shot rang out, smashing through the window to Lena's left and narrowly missing them all, before going out of the open window to Vincenzo's right.

'I should have asked for a gun,' Lena

said to no one in particular.

'I thought so too,' said Sister Dominique, pulling a handgun from her voluminous habit and handing it to Lena. 'So, I got us one each. You take the left and I'll take the right.' She pulled out another handgun. 'Vincenzo, you keep driving.'

'Yes, Sister Dominique.'

Lena wound her window down and leaned out, uncertain if she would be hit at any time. People were running out of the way of both the truck and any shots that fired out. They were on an open boulevard, which had a central reservation, covered in flowers.

It took Lena a while to realise that the shots were coming from a car on the opposite carriageway. It was driving against the traffic on that side. She had to pull back sharply when she realised that someone in the back seat had a gun pointed right at her. Then she saw that the person — she thought it was a man, but was not sure — had to reload. She took that moment to aim at the car's front tire, and take a shot. She missed and cried 'Damn!'

She tried again, just as she saw that her assailant had finished loading their gun, and this time her bullet hit the tire, causing the car to swerve and plough straight into a lamppost. She would not kill a person, as it went against everything she believed in, but she had no qualms about a rubber tire dying for the good of all.

'Well done!' she heard Greg call from the back.

'Are the children alright?' she called back.

'They're scared, but OK. Tell Vincenzo to head for the San Martinez Road.'

'I heard,' Vincenzo nodded. 'It is too narrow for other cars. First, we have to get there.'

'Where are the resistance?' Lena asked. 'They were supposed to be following us.'

'Gregori thought they might attract more attention,' Sister Dominique said. 'So, he called them off. He has them waiting on the south coast, at the hangar, in case we meet trouble there.'

'We're in trouble here,' Lena said, as another shot rang out. Her heart was racing. She had never known excitement like it. Adrenalin was telling her it was thrilling, but her rational brain was telling her that no one could live like this all the time. She wondered why they were so set on stopping the Count leaving. Surely the big prize was the king and queen? She had very little time to think about it, when another shot rang out, this time from someone on a motorcycle on the other carriageway.

The rider was too fast for her to be able to get the wheels. It nipped in and out of traffic much better than they did, and took a zigzag route, making it harder for her to focus on one spot.

They drove at speed out of the city, and into the countryside, before coming to a smaller town. All the time, shots rang out, and Lena began to fear they were more exposed, until they reached the township, which, compared to the vast city of Caria, was like a village, albeit a sprawling one.

Twice she tried to shoot the bike wheels and twice she failed. It was some comfort that the rider struggled to control the bike and shoot, meaning that most of their shots went wide. Lena guessed that it was less about shooting them and more about seeing where they went.

'We're coming up on San Martinez Road,' Vincenzo said. 'Everybody brace.'

Lena could see the road sign ahead of them on the right. It would mean having to go across the front of the bike. For a moment, Lena thought Vincenzo was going to go past, but instead he only turned onto the road at the very last minute, giving the rider no time to react.

'Brace!' he called.

Lena prayed that Greg had heard him, when they sped across the carriageway, where she was satisfied to see the rider's look of shock. She heard a loud crack and looked back just long enough to see the bike on its side, its wheels spinning and its rider unseated and obviously unconscious. She heard a cheer from the trailer.

San Martinez Road was so narrow, even the truck struggled to get through. It had obviously been built in the time before motor vehicles. The houses had overhanging upper floors on either side, which meant they almost touched.

When they were halfway through, Greg banged the roof twice. It was their agreed sign that Vincenzo was to stop. He put the brakes on and the truck lurched to a stop.

'We walk from here,' Greg said, having jumped down from the back and opened Lena's door. It only just opened wide enough for her to get out. 'They'll be looking for the truck with two nuns now.'

Lena jumped out, followed by Sister Dominique. The Count jumped down, helped by his grandson, and the children were helped down just after. Vincenzo came around to the front of the truck, where they joined him.

'That was rather thrilling!' Rachel said, her eyes shining.

'It was very noisy,' said Reuben. 'I don't like noise.' His breathing was more laboured than before and his face was pale.

'We'll be somewhere quiet soon,' Lena soothed him. She took both their hands.

'We can cut through the bazaar,' Greg said. 'Vincenzo, you go the other way and keep out of sight. One of them might have seen you and try to get information.'

'They won't get any from me, sir,' said Vincenzo.

'We won't forget what you've done for us,' said the Count, shaking Vincenzo's hand.

'I look forward to when we can meet again in free Cariastan,' said Vincenzo.

The Count appeared to swallow hard, his face a wave of emotion. 'We will not abandon you, my friend. But I must take this journey, you understand?'

Vincenzo nodded.

'I'll return in a week or so,' Greg promised. 'Lena, Sister Dominique, I think you should leave the habits here.'

164

Lena was relieved to take off the habit. Her sweater stuck to her body, but as she was only wearing a bra underneath, she could not take that off. Sister Dominique took off her own habit, somewhat reluctantly, to reveal she wore a long-sleeved white blouse and a black mid-length skirt.

'Now, we must go,' the Count said. 'It'll be night time soon.'

Greg and the Count had to leave their rifles with Vincenzo, as they could not be seen carrying large weapons in a public place, but like Lena and Sister Dominique, they had handguns, which they concealed under their clothes. Lena held Reuben's hand, and the sister held Rachel's.

They ducked into the cool, dim bazaar, which covered the length of the road leading to the docks. Brightly coloured goods filled every stall, including silk scarves and every type of clothing and accessory, Persian rugs, and fine china, painted in deep dark reds and azure blues. Aromas filled the air, from the street cafes, selling coffee and various roasted and fried meats and vegetables. Despite having eaten at the convent — and Rachel had been right about the carrots — Lena's mouth watered when they passed a stall where plump chickens turned on a rotisserie and sliced potatoes coated in paprika, were being fried in a large cauldron style pot.

Barkers called out their wares, along with prices. She had no idea how much a Cariastan shilling was in English money, but she would have happily spent quite a few of them. Not for the first time Lena wished she had more chance to explore this beautiful country. She vowed to return one day, when the war was over, and have her fill of it all. It felt like a place one could explore forever and still not know completely.

As they walked through the bazaar, she could not strike off the feeling that they were being watched. Her heart had only just got back to a normal rhythm after their dramatic race to get there, but she knew they were still in danger and would be until they could leave Cariastan.

They came out of the other side of the bazaar. The sun had begun to set in the west, but it was still warm, and Lena felt that now familiar prickly heat under her sweater.

The docks were just a couple of hundred meters away, through the outside market. There were more market stalls, selling fresh food and fresh fish, the aromas filling the cool night air. People still shopped, even this late in the day, buying meat and fish to take home for supper. But they had all come to a standstill, with dozens looking out over the sea, and talking in hushed voices.

'What it is?' the Count asked.

'Dear God,' said Greg, astounded.

Lena followed their glances, and gasped.

A couple of miles out to sea, coming from the northwest, was what appeared to be a dark mass.

'What is it?' asked Rachel. 'Why is everyone stopping?'

Greg had not stopped. He was pushing through the crowd. The others followed him, until they were nearer to the dockside, but still hidden amongst the stalls.

'We can't go,' said the Count, when they had stopped. 'Not now. We can't leave Cariastan to those monsters.'

'We have to, Grandpa,' said Greg. 'We made a promise to Sister Dominique, to these children — and to the king.'

'The king would understand.'

'He needs us to do this. We can return when our task is over,' Greg argued. 'Don't forget that Lena did not sign up for this.'

'Don't worry about me,' Lena said. 'I came knowing the dangers, and I am fully with you in this fight.'

'Thank you.' Greg looked at her for what seemed a long time.

She would have liked to tell him just how much staying with him meant to her. It had only been a very short time, but she already felt a deep connection to him and to his country. She had almost forgotten Polly Smith and her original reason for tagging along. All that seemed a long way away, in the past. They were dealing with the now, and how to stay alive long enough to get the Count, Sister Dominique and the children to safety. She thought about her grandmother's echoes from the past, including Polly and Clara, and already knew that these people with whom she had undertaken such a hazardous journey would echo throughout her life.

'We do have to get to England,' Greg said. 'We'll have to find another route to the plane. Not only that, but we have to get in the air before they get further south.' He nodded towards the boats out at sea. 'They won't stop here.'

Sister Dominique put her hand on the Count's arm, because he looked as if he might argue. 'We have to get to her,' she whispered. 'Then we can decide what to do next.'

'What is it?' asked Reuben, echoing his sister. He sounded tired. 'What is everyone looking at?' He stood on tiptoes.

Lena looked out again, at the dark, sinister mass in the distance, while trying to work out why Sister Dominique was so invested in getting the Count away from Cariastan and back to his wife. The heat had left her body to be replaced by an icy finger of fear running down her spine.

'They're German gunboats, Reuben,' said Greg, his mouth set in a thin line. 'And they're blocking off the channel.'

17

1890

Polly ran a damp cloth over Anton's head. He lay back on the pillow, his chest bare, as they had to undress him to cool the fever. His black hair was tousled, and damp. He had been semiconscious for several days. The ship's doctor had diagnosed food poisoning.

'It is still touch and go,' said Doctor Hernandez. 'He will need constant nursing.'

'I'll stay with him,' said Polly. Before the doctor left the cabin, Polly drew him back. 'Are you sure it was food poisoning? There was a man who was allowed to board the ship the night before last. I didn't realise until after Anton collapsed, but I am sure now that I saw him coming into this cabin with a tray of food. I thought he was a porter, but now I worry . . .'

'Where is the tray?' Doctor Hernandez looked around the cabin.

'Erm, I don't know. Unless it was removed before Anton took ill.'

'It would be difficult to diagnose without having a sample. Do you know why anyone would attempt such a thing?'

Polly almost told him about her own brush with death, but she was afraid it would sound fantastical. 'I don't know yet, but it's connected to other events,' was all she said.

As if realising she was not willing to say more, the doctor had left her with Anton.

That had been two days ago. He called back a couple of times a day to check on the patient, but said to Polly. 'All we need now is time. The young man obviously has a strong constitution.'

The rest of the time, Polly was alone with Anton. Eddie and Violet had put their heads around the door a couple of times to check on her and try to coax her out for some food, but she refused. She was terrified that if she left him again, some harm would come to him.

'Polly,' he whispered as she wiped his brow.

'Yes, Anton?' Her heart quickened.

'Polly, I am sorry.'

'What for? You nearly died.' Tears stung her eyes. The thought of losing him cut deep and painfully.

'Maybe it is what I deserved. I thought it would be so easy. A bit of fun even. And then you happened. You were not supposed to be there, my Boudicca with her red hair . . .'

'What are you talking about, Anton?'

'It is a mess,' he said, as if not hearing her properly. 'I do not know how to put it right.'

'Shhh,' she soothed. 'You've done nothing wrong, my love.' The endearment came out before she could stop herself.

'I tried to keep away from you,' he said. 'It made me more miserable than I can ever say. Whatever happens, remember that I love you.'

She kissed his forehead, tenderly. 'And

I love you, too.'

Despite their mutual declaration, the words felt more like goodbye. An unexpected tear fell from her eye. Anton drifted back off, leaving Polly feeling as though the heart she had given to him had been torn in two, but for what reason she could not say.

By the time they reached Cariastan, he was up and about, though still very pale. Polly had helped him dress in silence. If he remembered what he had said while delirious, he was keeping it to himself. Their relationship took on a formal tone.

'Thank you for taking care of me,' he said, as she helped him to button his coat.

'I'd do it for anyone,' she tried to say breezily.

'Yes, I know you would. Polly . . .'

'Yes?'

'There's something I need to talk to you about before we disembark.'

'What is it? Are you still poorly? I can speak to the Ambassador and tell him you're not well enough.'

174

'No, I'm not ill. I just . . .' He ran his hands through his hair in a way that had become familiar to her. 'Oh, it is a mess!'

'You said that while you were half-asleep.' Polly handed him a comb for his hair.

'The thing is . . .'

He was interrupted by a knock on the door. It was one of the porters.

'The carriage from Caria is here,' he said. 'The ambassador has asked that you hurry. He said Miss Harrington is becoming concerned.'

'Of course,' said Anton. 'We're coming now.'

'I'll go and get my things,' Polly said, leaving him, and silently cursing the porter for interrupting them. Something was preying on Anton's mind and she wanted to know what it was.

They met up at the carriage, and rode in silence to Caria. He seemed to have shrunk into a corner, as if hiding in the dark. They passed a market place and what appeared to be a long, covered bazaar. She put it on the mental list of things that she wanted to explore about Cariastan when she had the chance.

The carriage went up a narrow road called San Martinez, where the houses on either side almost met at the top. One could almost step from one balcony onto the one opposite. Once they had come to the end of that road, they turned out into the open countryside, which was lush and green, with rich crops of wheat and some orange groves. Far ahead in the distance, she could see the tell-tale lines of vineyards in the foothills of the mountain. The mountain itself stretched high into a white peak, but she was not sure if it was snow or the colour of the rocks.

They reached the city about an hour later, and the carriage pulled into an archway leading to the ambassador's sprawling white villa. The gardens bloomed with flowers of all colours and a fountain in the centre splashed cooling water into a pond, where large goldfish swam.

'It's just lovely,' said Polly.

To her surprise they pulled up at the front doors, rather than going around to the back, which servants usually used. Perhaps, she thought, that's how it was in Cariastan.

'Come on,' said Anton, when they got out of the carriage. 'Let's get this over with.' He had become cold, almost savage in his tone, yet a muscle twitching on his jawline suggested he was holding back a deep emotion.

The doors opened and a butler came out. 'We are so relieved to see you return, Sir,' he said, bowing to Anton.

Polly knew then what was coming next, and if she was honest with herself, she had always suspected. He had never truly behaved like a servant. Or at least not like any she had ever known. It still took the breath from her lungs to hear the butler say it out loud.

'Welcome back, Count Gregori. Your fiancé awaits you in the conservatory.'

17

The ambassador had told Clara the truth in the days after their arrival in Cariastan. At first, she was relieved that the meeting had been prorogued. It gave her time to catch her breath and calm herself. This turned to offence when he still failed to arrive back to meet her.

'He wanted to do his part in making sure Miss Smith was safe,' the ambassador explained.

Clara might not have been worldly, but neither was she naïve. She immediately distrusted Anton's intentions in staying with Polly. Men who were engaged to be married should not show interest in other women, even if that marriage was one of convenience and had been arranged when they were children.

By the time he arrived back in Cariastan, she was seething with fury, not least because she realised that Polly was going to be hurt and that she would be the cause of that pain.

She waited in the conservatory, where Mrs Lovett sat in a corner, feigning interest in a book. Clara was sure that they would both come to her. She was dismayed when only Anton entered.

He looked very pale and drawn. News of his food poisoning had reached them, and while Clara did not wish ill on him, she was also angry enough to believe that a few days ill-health served him right!

He opened his mouth to speak, then closed it again. 'Nothing I say is going to make this right, is it?' he eventually said.

'I swear to God,' Clara said, holding herself rigid, 'If you have done anything to disgrace her.'

Anton held up his hand. 'Dear Lord, no. You have my word on that. I care about her too much to do that.'

Clara glanced at Mrs Lovett, before moving closer to Anton and murmuring. 'You love her? Before you reply, be assured you will not be breaking my heart by saying so. I am not even sure I like you very much at the moment.'

'Yes. I love her. It was not meant to be that way. I only came to England to get to know you. From childhood I have been told who I am to marry, and I have tried to be true to that. I don't say I have been an angel in my young life. I did not know you. Then I met her, and when someone tried to kill her, I swore to myself I would do anything to protect her. Even then, I told myself I was doing it for you. Taking care of your good friend. I only denied the truth to myself — that I was already in love with her.'

'Why not just come to England as yourself? Why the subterfuge? How can I be expected to trust anything you say, when you have deceived both of us? How do I know that you did not just think you would have some last-minute fun with someone you only saw as a servant girl?'

Anton looked at her levelly. 'You know she is so much more than that.'

'Yes, I know she is. I just want to be sure you do,' Clara countered.

'I have no intention of breaking my promise to you,' Anton said. 'I am not that much of a cad. When you wrote to me, telling me of your predicament, I promised I would help you escape your life in England by keeping the promise our parents made, and I will.'

'Or perhaps you just think she's beneath you.'

'Again, you know that is not true. She is better than anyone I have ever met. I only came as a servant because I did not want all the pomp and circumstance that usually goes around a visit from the nobility. I wanted to see things as they really were, not as your aunt and uncle pretended them to be.'

Clara ran a hand across her clammy forehead. 'I cannot return to that house,' she said. 'I need this marriage if I am to have some kind of independence. We have created a legal and binding contract to marry. I warn you that if we do marry, you will not take her as your mistress. Any other woman, yes. I am not so naïve as to believe that such cold-blooded alliances lead to true contentment and fidelity. But not her. Never her. I won't have you ruining her reputation. Do you know if she loves you?'

'Yes, I believe she does.'

'Oh, God, what a mess,' Clara said, feeling tears prick her eyes. She swallowed back a lump in her throat. 'She has been my best friend since childhood, and yet she will hate me now.'

'I don't think she could ever hate you.'

'Where is she?'

'She's gone to your room to make sure they have unpacked things properly for you.'

'I will go and speak to her, and try to make her understand. I hate this situation,' Clara said. 'I hate my own selfishness. At the moment, future husband, I hate you, so perhaps you would be so good as to give me a wide berth for a few days.'

When she saw the anguish in his eyes, she knew it was not for what he had lost with her. It was for what he had lost with Polly. Clara was not one to be deliberately cruel, no matter how angry she was. 'I appreciate that whatever else you may have done, you have at least been honest with me now. I am sorry for your pain, but this is the hand we have been dealt and we must go forward as best we can.'

Clara left him and went up to her room. Mrs Lovett followed, but when Clara reached her bedroom door, she waved her away. 'I am not planning to allow men into my room, Mrs Lovett,' she said, in harsher tones than she intended. 'I do thank you for your diligence,' she added quickly. 'But Polly can take care of me from here. You go and rest. We have the gala dinner tonight.'

She opened the bedroom door and walked in to see Polly standing near to the armoire, with her back to her. Polly had already changed back into her normal workaday wear of a plain black dress with starched white collar and cuffs. Her red hair had been pulled back into a tight bun.

'Polly,' Clara said. She wanted to hug her friend, but was afraid. 'Polly, I'm so sorry!'

Polly turned around, with a big smile

on her face. 'I'm just sorting out which of your clothes need cleaning and pressing. They obviously want organising properly. I can't find anything. What are you wearing to the dinner tonight?' It was as if she had not even heard Clara's apology, as she ploughed on, chatting away nine to the dozen. 'The cook, Fatima, tells me it's going to be wonderful, based on Arabian recipes. Lots of lamb and dates. I'm sure you will love it. So, which dress do you want, Miss Clara?'

Clara winced when she heard Polly addressing her so formerly. 'You don't have to call me Miss Clara now, Polly. Not now that we're away from there.'

'Actually,' Polly said, blinking rapidly, 'I think I should. They're a bit more formal here, and we can't be too careful. Plus, you'll be a Countess soon, and it wouldn't look right for me to address you by your first name. I am just a servant after all,' she said stiffly.

'Polly, I didn't know it was him. Honestly, I would never have put you in that position.'

'Oh, the Count? He's a card, isn't he?' Polly laughed, but there was a brittle bitterness to it. 'He must have thought it was right funny, pretending to be a servant. I wondered why he never actually ever seemed to do any proper work. He was rubbish at ironing. Speaking of which, I'll just take your things to be pressed. I'll come back in a while and run your bath, Miss Clara.'

Polly rushed past Clara as if she had the hounds of hell behind her, sweeping out of the room with an armful of clothes.

Clara could only watch her go, struck with the painful realisation that they would never be friends and confidantes again.

18

It occurred to Lena that anyone searching the barn for them would immediately hear Rueben's laboured breathing. There was nothing they could do about it. She could not ask the little boy to hold his breath.

They had been there for four hours. Greg had managed to buy them the chicken and potatoes from the market, along with bottles of mineral water from a café along the coast. Lena had longed to taste the food, and she was sure that on any other occasion it would taste like nectar. Unfortunately, nerves had left her mouth arid, and this affected her taste buds. She ate only because she knew she had to, not because the food was delicious. Sister Dominique and Rachel had eaten heartily, the Count had tried, but seemed to have lost his appetite. Reuben had struggled with a few mouthfuls, before suffering from a hacking cough, and Greg had shaken his head when offered his share.

'You must keep your strength up,' Lena chided him, gently. 'We need you to fly us out of here.'

She shifted in the hay. In films, it always looked so romantic, when a man and woman were lying back in a haystack, giving way to their feelings. The reality was a musty smell and sharp ends sticking through the fibres of your clothing.

'I'll get you home, don't worry,' Greg promised.

'I know you will,' she said. 'I have every faith in you.' His face was drawn and watchful.

'How are the *Caria* and *Dominique* going to get through the German blockade?' the Count asked.

Lena was struck by something, and wanted to ask a question, but before she could put it into words, Greg replied to his grandfather. 'They won't. They'll probably have to go south too. We have to find a way to let people know. I should have flown further north.'

'You did what you thought was right,' his grandfather said.

'Shhh,' said Sister Dominique. 'Someone is coming.' They quickly switched off the torches they had been holding.

They were on the upper floor of the barn. They all lay flat, but in the silence, Reuben's breathing was louder than ever. 'I'm sorry,' he said, when Lena put her hand on his back to steady him.

She wanted to put her arms around him and tell him it did not matter, but any movement might alert someone below. She shook her head and mouthed 'It's OK,' hoping it was enough to let him know he owed them no apology.

The barn door opened, and even Reuben seemed to hold his breath as they heard movement in the stalls beneath them. Someone was shining a torch into every stall, as if searching.

'Gregori,' a voice hissed. 'Gregori, where are you, man?'

'Ivan?' Greg crawled to the ladder and looked over. 'Ivan, you old . . .' He appeared to stop himself, as if remembering there were children in the area. 'What took you so long?' It was not said in anger, only urgency. He turned on his torch and shone it down to his friend.

'We had a bit of a skirmish with some collaborators.'

'I thought you looked a bit rough,' said Greg, climbing down the ladder.

Lena peered over and saw that Ivan's hair was tousled and he had dark stains, of either blood or bruises, on his forehead and cheek.

'You should see the other guy,' he quipped. 'We've got some transport for you, but you must hurry. The Germans are starting to move south, as well as coming from the sea.'

Greg beckoned to the others to join him on the ground floor. Lena helped the children down, then the sister and the Count.

They all went outside, into the dark farmyard, where a coach awaited them.

It was a school bus and said White Peak Academy on the side.

'Won't that be a bit obvious, at night?' Greg asked. 'No schools are open this late.'

'Believe me, friend,' said Ivan. 'Nothing is going to be obvious. You're not the only people travelling south since the blockade arrived. The *Caria* and *Dominique* have sent word that they are redirecting there. We're evacuating as many as we can. People are travelling by car, horse, cart, bus, truck, on foot — any way they can get away.'

'Good,' the Count said, cutting in. 'Now let's go, before we lose our chance.'

They all climbed onto the bus. Lena breathed a sigh of relief when she saw two oxygen canisters tucked into one of the overhead luggage racks. She settled Reuben in and then, when everyone else was on board, and Ivan had started the engine, she took one down and set it up, before putting a mask on the child.

After a few minutes, his laboured breathing eased and he settled back and shut his eyes. She sat next to him, to keep an eye on the oxygen levels, while Greg and his grandfather took one seat, and Rachel sat huddled up to Sister Dominique. The little girl's love of adventure seemed to have subsided in the face of genuine danger. Her eyes were large and watchful, and became even more concerned whenever she looked at her brother.

As they drove through the countryside, they saw dozens of people walking in the same direction as them, carrying everything they owned on carts. Children sat on the carts, or were carried on their parents' backs.

'We should let some on,' Lena told Greg. 'it feels wrong that we can sit comfortably while they struggle.'

He nodded. 'Ivan, you heard the lady. We can take at least another dozen people.'

The moment Ivan stopped, the coach was surrounded with desperate people, begging a lift. Greg stood at the doors, and as they surged forward said, 'We are sorry, we can only take a dozen of you.' He paused and looked up the bus. 'Maybe a few more if people don't mind standing.'

When he stood back, the crowd surged forward, piling onto the bus in much higher figures than he had said. By the time they had finished, some seats held three people and there were about eight people standing, including some children, and parents holding babes in arms. The noise was a cacophony, and it disturbed Reuben, who became alarmed at the sudden influx of people.

'Enough!' Greg shouted, holding his arm across the entrance. 'Ivan, shut the door!'

Ivan pressed the button that closed the door, but even then, people tried to pile on. Finally, it closed, and they moved off, but some hung onto the running board, and Lena could hear people on the roof. Rachel started to cry, as Ivan sped up, and some people fell off onto the roadside, thankfully not hurt too badly.

'We can't take you all!' Greg said to

those standing, who had begun to complain because their families had been left behind. 'Don't you see? It's only a small bus. But we'll send it back for them, right Ivan?'

Ivan nodded. 'Yes, I'll come back, I promise.'

It stemmed some of the anger, but there was a definite tension in the air, despite the fact that they were helping those who had got on the bus to escape. There was no gratitude, only desperation and an apparent bitterness that they had transport in the first place. Part of the tension came from how closely people were crammed together. Lena felt as if she could hardly breathe. Fear had its own particular aroma and she thought she might choke on it if she did not get any air soon. She pulled back the small window opening, but it gave little respite from the crammed conditions.

Greg had to stay in the doorwell, because his seat next to his grandfather had been taken by a woman and child.

'You could get two children on that

seat next to the boy if you stand,' one man said to Lena.

'He's ill,' she said firmly, looking him direct in the eye. 'He has pneumonia. I'm his doctor and I am not leaving his side.' She hated being selfish, but Reuben was her main concern, and she would not be bullied by a man who thought he knew better.

That at least made him shut up and she was aware of people moving away from them a little, perhaps from fear of catching something. It gave Reuben more space and he began to relax again.

With so many people piled on it, the bus moved slower. This caused others who were walking to try to stop it to get a lift. Whenever that happened, Ivan would speed up a little, but it was not enough to make good ground, and the hordes of people moving south had a tendency to use all the road. She did not blame them, nor hate them for their desperation. She only wished the bus could go quicker, so they could get off and she could breathe fresh air again.

Eventually the tension in the bus seemed to ease a little, perhaps because the new people on it began to understand how it felt to be the ones with transport while so many walked. The guilt of surviving became a shared experience.

'Excuse me,' said the woman sitting next to the Count. She was about twenty-six years old, with olive skin and dark hair. A widow's peak on her forehead gave her the look of an immortal being, brought down from Olympus to live among humans. 'Would the little boy and girl like some grapes? They're from my family's vineyard.'

Rachel took some, but Reuben only shook his head and closed his eyes again, whispering, 'No, thank you,' through his mask.

'Where is the vineyard?' asked the Count.

'In the foothills, below the White Peak,' the woman said.

'Is that the Garibaldi place?'

'Yes, that is right. I am Selena Garibaldi and this little fella is my son,

Benjamin.'

'My wife and I have enjoyed your wine for many years,' said the Count. 'In fact, old Alberto Garibaldi once helped to save my wife's life.'

'Grandfather . . . ' Greg said, warily.

'What? Oh. I see.' The Count looked at Lena and smiled. 'Well, Selena Garibaldi, I am glad to at last pay my debt to Alberto by helping you get to safety. I pray we all make it.'

'Did your wife fall off White Peak?' Rachel asked. Lena could have kissed the little girl, because it was what she wanted to know, though she might not have asked in those terms.

The bus became silent, as if everyone wanted to know the answer to that question.

'I don't think it's appropriate in front of the children,' Sister Dominique interrupted. 'Especially not in front of Rachel and Reuben.'

Lena became convinced that even if the rest of the bus did not say a disappointed 'aw', they were all thinking it.

196

Even Reuben, who had until then had his eyes closed, had come to attention.

'I think it would be rather nice to hear a story about someone who fell off the White Peak and then lived,' said Rachel. 'She is alive, isn't she?'

'Yes, the Countess is alive,' Lena said. 'I met her in London.'

'I should like to meet her too,' said Rachel. 'She sounds very brave.'

'She was the bravest woman I have ever known,' said the Count. He shrugged at his grandson in a rather gallic fashion. 'Since I appear to have a captive audience, and Doctor Turner wants answers, I think a further chapter of the story is in order.'

19

The days that followed Clara's arrival in Cariastan, and Anton's return, were supposed to be filled with a never-ending cycle of lunches, balls and fetes in their honour. Clara had refused all invitations, and even refused to appear at the gala dinner. Anton had sent the excuse that he was still recovering from his journey, so that no blame fell upon Clara. He told her he owed her that much. They were due to make their marriage official in the cathedral on the second Saturday of the following month.

On the few times they went out together in his coach, to take part in pre-nuptial rehearsals, she came across as the blushing bride-to-be and he thc handsome Count who had found himself an English Rose. Both were far too well brought up to pretend to be anything else. They waved and smiled, but at no point did they engage with others.

She could pretend from a distance, where people could not see her face close up, but she struggled to smile and make polite conversation with others in private. She had been there a week, and very few people in Cariastan had seen anything of her, other than a pale profile, half obscured by the frame on the carriage windows and the large brim of her bonnet.

She at least gave Anton credit for not trying to romance her in the times they were alone together. He did not try to appease her, nor flirt. He was always polite and attentive, ensuring she was not too cold or too hot, or that she had eaten well enough. But it was all done as if she were a guest who would be leaving soon, not the woman who was about to share his life and perhaps even his children.

In private, they spent very little time together. They separated the moment they returned from anywhere, and dined alone in their rooms when possible. The ambassador acted as a medium, and appeared aware of the problems they faced.

Clara was not heartbroken and angry that he had fallen in love with Polly. There was no sexual or romantic jealousy involved. She was heartbroken and angry that his subterfuge had cost her the best friend she had ever known.

Whatever feelings Polly had, she hid behind a brittle, cheerful tone as she helped Clara to dress in the mornings and undress in the evenings. There were times, in the past, they would find excuses to spend time together, such as Polly sitting darning Clara's petticoats while she worked on her needlepoint, but those days had gone. The atmosphere between them was too awkward for Clara to even suggest it.

There was so much she had not shared with Polly, including that apparent attempt on her own life and what she had learned about her parents' death. If Anton had fallen in love with any other woman but Polly, she would have shared that too.

Instead, she found herself too often in the company of Mrs Lovett, which was not the same.

'Do you like to read?' Clara asked her chaperone one day, when they had no engagements. They were in Clara's sitting room, which overlooked the exotic gardens of the villa. The French doors were wide open and a soft breeze blew from the mountains.

'Oh no, Miss Clara. Reading is not a good pastime for young women. It can be distressing for them to read about exciting adventures.'

'I have read lots of adventures and yet here I am,' said Clara.

'Hopefully, when you are married, you will have no need for such fantasies.'

'Everyone needs a fantasy, Mrs Lovett,' Clara said. 'When Polly and I were young we . . .' She stopped. Her chaperone would not understand.

'I am glad you mentioned your maid, Miss Clara. I hate to be indelicate, but

I am aware of . . . certain events. I have been discreet, of course. It is none of my business. Under the circumstances, and if you wish your marriage to work, might it not be better to send her back to England before you are married? It would not be proper for her to attend your wedding, as I believe you had planned for her to do.'

It occurred to Clara that Mrs Lovett was right. It was the most obvious answer to the whole problem. She would not have to live with the guilt of seeing Polly every day, knowing that her friend was in love with her husband and he with her — because no matter how much Polly tried to pretend all was normal, Clara knew it was not and that it never would be again. Their friendship was damaged beyond repair, and all they had now was their professional relationship and even that was stilted and uncomfortable. They had lost that bond they had shared since they were little girls.

'If you're going downstairs for your walk,' Clara said. 'Could you call into the kitchens and ask Polly to come and see me?'

If Mrs Lovett was annoyed at being dismissed so casually, she said nothing. She simply smiled and said, 'Anything to help you, Miss Clara. I want you to know how fond of you I have become.'

'And I of you,' Clara said. The words were automatic. The sort of thing one says not because it's true, but because it's obviously expected. The truth was, she barely knew Mrs Lovett, and guiltily, realised she had not really tried to get to know her. 'We should go out together one day,' Clara said. 'I am thinking of visiting the convent. Would you like to accompany me? Not as my chaperone, but as my friend.'

'I should be delighted, Miss Clara,' said Mrs Lovett. 'Then, perhaps we can go and visit the White Peak, which I am told is only a few hundred yards further up the mountain. I have been told the views down over the valley are rather pleasing.'

'The White Peak . . .' Clara paused.

Did she want to go there? Perhaps she did. Perhaps it was what she needed to finally lay her parents to rest. 'I will think on it,' she said. 'Please send Polly to me. I will be in my bedroom.'

★ ★ ★

Polly was in the kitchen with Fatima, the cook and Mohammed, the gardener. They were a married couple who ran the ambassador's villa like clockwork.

Fatima had made Polly the strongest, sweetest coffee she had ever tasted, serving it in a tiny cup, painted in bright and rich blues and reds.

'It's delicious,' Polly said.

'It is how we make it at home,' Fatima explained. 'Not weak coffee the English make.'

'How did you come to Cariastan?' Polly asked. Fatima was rolling out pastry. That too was unlike anything Polly had ever known, so thin that one could see through it. Fatima used some filled with lamb and aubergines in a rich sauce, then others she filled with apples and dates. Both were scrumptious and the pastry melted in the mouth. Polly felt a sudden urge to tell Bessie all about it.

'We had to flee our land due to religious persecution,' Fatima explained. 'The ambassador welcomed us here, and allowed us to continue in our own faith.'

Polly was missing her friends in England more than she ever thought she could. She felt as if she had no one now. True, Fatima and Mohammed were warm and welcoming, but she had known them only a week or so. She no longer had Clara to turn to. She was alone in a strange country, with no one to share her new experiences with.

Despite her resolve to stay calm and pretend she did not care about Anton, her heart, which she had given to him completely, was broken. She did not blame Clara, but that did not stop the resentment building. It only served to highlight the gulf between them — which had always been between them, had Polly not fooled herself into thinking their different social statuses did not matter. It did matter and it always had.

Even if Clara was not marrying the man that Polly was in love with, it was unlikely that any man of high standing would put up with her being best friends with a maid. She realised that the only reason the Harringtons had allowed it was because having Polly as a friend stopped Clara from seeking friendship elsewhere, with people who might make her see how lonely and isolated her life was. Then, for some reason, they had tried to put an end to that connection. Where they had failed, Anton had succeeded, whether he meant to or not.

She drank her coffee and looked at the invitation that had been sent in her name.

Polly,

Come and see us as soon as you can. We're staying at the Scheherazade.

Your friends,

Eddie and Vi Shirebrook

There was so much to do for Clara's wedding. She barely had time to reply.

She would make time, as soon as Clara was on her honeymoon.

'Miss Harrington wants to see you,' said a voice from the door. It was Mrs Lovett. 'She's in her room.'

'Thank you,' said Polly, getting up.

'Take her some pastries,' Fatima said. 'The young lady is too thin.'

'I don't think that's your business,' said Mrs Lovett, pursing her lips. 'Hurry up, Polly. She's waiting.' As Polly brushed past her, she murmured, loud enough to be heard, 'These foreigners, sticking their nose in.'

'They're good, hardworking people,' Polly said.

'Well, they're your kind, aren't they?' Mrs Lovett said. 'It's always best not to try to rise above one's station.'

Polly gave her a long, hard look. When had the inobtrusive Mrs Lovett suddenly become so waspish? Was it because of Anton? She supposed that there would be disapproval from people who thought Polly was getting above herself.

'I think,' said Mrs Lovett, as Polly

walked away, 'that you might be better returning to England.'

Polly spun around. 'I really think that's none of your business,' she said, rattled by how close to her own thoughts Mrs Lovett had come.

The woman walked towards her, as she stood at the bottom of the back staircase, unable to move. 'As I said, dear, you are getting ideas above your station. I may only be a chaperone, but I am a lady of genteel background. You are a maid and indeed, I hear, the child of a woman of ill-repute.'

As she spoke, she looked up and smiled slightly.

Polly's cheeks were flaming as she began to turn. How could Clara have told Mrs Lovett that secret about her mother? The memory of her mother and her profession as an actress, which, in the public's minds was synonymous with being a fallen woman, was something that Polly had shared with very few other people. She faced the stairs and looked up, ready to begin her ascent, only to see

Anton standing there, his face a mask of anger.

'Excuse me, sir,' she said, brushing past him, her heart pounding in her chest.

As she did, she heard him say in mild, but cold tones, 'A word, Mrs Lovett, please.'

She fought to temptation to eavesdrop on their conversation. No doubt he was trying to find out more about her mother. Her mother's profession had never bothered her as much as it did in that moment. Few children from the orphanage came from good homes. That was the point of them being there, as the various so-called Christian matrons who passed through on a regular basis liked to remind them. They were repeatedly told that they had been born from sin, and that this would probably taint them all their lives.

Polly had learned to dismiss it as nonsense, thanks to the love of Bessie Cooper and the friendship of Clara. Mrs Lovett's disapproving words had brought it all

back. All the shame, all the embarrass-
ment, all the inherited sin. She had been
told by one matron that she would never
get to heaven, because there was too
much of her mother in her. 'It's this red
hair,' the matron said, cutting it all off
in a fit of anger over some transgression
that Polly had long since forgotten. What
she had not forgotten were the scissors
scratching her scalp, and how mortified
she had been by the uneven mess left.
'Only a woman of ill-repute would have
hair of this colour,' the matron had said.
'And she has passed that sin on to you.'

As an adult, Polly had rationalised
it all, and learned to accept that the
matron's prejudices had nothing to do
with Christianity or goodness. When she
first went to Derwent Priory, her hair
was still an uneven mess, so Bessie had
gently trimmed it, all the time hissing
under her breath at the sort of monster
who would hurt a child.

'Don't you hide your light under a
bushel,' Bessie had said. 'God gave you
this hair, just as he gave life to your

poor dear mother. You've nothing to be ashamed of, and neither did she if all she wanted was to put food on your table.'

Back then, Polly had not been in love nor had ever imagined being in love. Now, with Anton learning the truth of her background, all that shame came flooding back. No decent man would want a woman with such a past in his household. Did she want to stay anyway? Life had become more difficult. Clara no longer confided in her, and she no longer felt comfortable enough to share below stairs gossip, which Clara had always enjoyed hearing. Polly had never been unkind about her fellow servants, but she did very good impressions of Bessie, Mr Turner and Mrs Jenkins that had often left Clara in fits of laughter.

By the time she reached Clara's bedroom, Polly's mind was made up.

'Ah, there you are, Polly,' Clara said. She sat at the dressing table, her gaze fixed upon the mirror. She did not turn around, nor did she make any attempt to look at Polly's reflection in the mirror.

She stared straight ahead. 'I needed to talk to you about your future here.'

'I'm glad you've said that, Miss Clara,' Polly said, rapidly. 'I've come to the decision that I think it's best if I go back to England. To be honest, it's too hot for me here, and I miss my friends, and you won't need me when you're a married woman. And I really think it's for the best.' The words tumbled out, leaving her breathless.

'Oh . . . ' Clara put her hands in her lap and clasped them together. 'I see. Yes, actually I was about to suggest the same thing. It was very selfish of me to bring you away from all the people you love.'

I loved you, Polly thought. *You were my best friend and now we won't be friends ever again.* She said none of this out loud. 'Well, you wanted a familiar face around, didn't you? But now you're getting to know everyone and you have Mrs Lovett.'

'Oh yes, Mrs Lovett,' Clara said. 'She's not the most exciting companion. I am sure you and I had better conversations about watching the paint dry when Uncle John had the hallway redecorated.'

They both laughed, and for a moment that connection was there again. The two lonely girls who could make each other laugh and forget the difficulties they each faced. Then it was gone, blown away on a breeze, like the seeds on a dandelion clock.

'I'll stay till after the wedding,' Polly said.

'Oh, no, there's no need. I think it best . . . I mean, well, there's a boat leaving on Friday, going back to England. There won't be another one for weeks. I thought it best if you caught the earlier one. If you wish to, of course. When you're no longer in my employment, it won't be my business.'

'Friday will be ideal,' said Polly. 'It's best I get off sooner rather than later, isn't it?'

'I think . . . yes . . . Polly?'

'Yes?'

'Thank you for everything.'

'It's been a pleasure, Miss Clara. Really. And I'm sorry for . . .'

Clara put up her hand. 'No, you've done nothing wrong. Nothing at all. I want you to know that. Now why don't you take the rest of the afternoon off? In fact, take the rest of the week off. Mrs Lovett can help me. You can go sightseeing. You said you wanted to see more of Cariastan.'

'You're dismissing me now?' asked Polly, feeling as if a door had just been slammed shut in her face.

'Just giving you a well-earned rest. I don't think you've ever had a holiday. Take one now and enjoy yourself.'

'Thank you. I'll come and say good-bye to you before I leave on Friday.'

'There's no need for that. I'm going up to the convent on Thursday to see Sister Marie Claire. I may stay there overnight. I hear there are rooms to rent. I think I need to be somewhere peaceful for a day or two.'

Polly opened her mouth to speak, then closed it again. She just nodded, not sure if Clara was even looking at her, because she continued to gaze resolutely into the mirror. This was it. The end of their friendship. There would not even be a proper goodbye.

'I'll leave you to it then.'

She turned and fled the room, running at full speed up to the servants' quarters, where she burst open her bedroom door and threw herself onto the bed.

20

'Is that when Polly left?' Lena asked. 'The Countess said that they broke up because of a man. That was you,' she said to the Count. She did not say it accusingly. She understood how difficult the situation had been. It sounded as if, apart from his silly scam of pretending to be a valet, he had behaved honourably to both women.

On the other hand, he was telling the story, so it was unlikely he would implicate himself in any wrongdoing. Even if he had been intent on seducing Polly, it seemed that she was certainly too honourable to deceive her friend.

The rest of the bus had listened, enraptured, by this tale of love and broken friendship from long ago.

'I don't understand,' said Rachel. 'Why was Polly's mum being an actress a bad thing?'

In his telling the Count had left out the part about actresses being synonymous with ill-repute at that time. He had known that most of his audience would understand, and he had not wanted to say too much in front of children.

'Actresses weren't very well thought of in the olden days,' Lena explained tactfully.

'The olden days,' the Count laughed. 'This is my younger days that we speak of. Please, less of this 'olden days'.'

'Is that why you didn't marry Polly?' Rachel asked. 'Because her mummy was an actress? I think that's awfully . . . awful of you.'

Sister Dominique had been silent through it all, but she suddenly spoke up. 'Rachel, it is not fair to judge the Count for judging Polly.' Her voice sounded sharper than usual. She softened it by adding, 'dearest'.

'What did you say to Mrs Lovett?' asked Rachel. 'I really don't like her. And yes, I know I am judging her, but she was mean to Polly and I like Polly. I think we should be allowed to judge people for being unkind.' She looked pointedly at Sister Dominique, who grinned back.

Murmurs of assent on the bus suggested that others agreed with her.

'Everybody liked Polly,' the Count said. 'It was impossible not to.'

'But now you love your wife?' asked Rachel.

'Yes, I love my wife with all my heart.'

'It's very sad and confusing,' the little girl said. 'Because Clara is very nice too and I think she deserves to be loved. Being grown up is rather difficult, isn't it?'

'Yes, little one,' said the Count. 'It is very difficult sometimes.'

'Well, I forgive you,' Rachel said. 'Because they're both such nice young ladies and both beautiful. You can't help what your heart does.'

Lena gave a rueful smile. For an eight-year-old, Rachel was incredibly wise. Life had made her so. At a time when she should be worried about nothing

218

more than what toys she wanted to play with and what she was going to wear to friends' birthday parties, she was on a packed bus escaping the German forces, with a twin brother who might not survive the journey.

She turned to Rueben and saw that he too was enthralled by everything. Perhaps this diversion from the present time was what they all needed. The tale of a love triangle from fifty years ago took their minds off what was happening outside the window. The stories people told each other, or the songs they sang, whether they be true or fictional, old or new, had always been the means of escape from life's horrors. It was why slaves and prisoners sang songs, and why bards told stories of men in green who stole from the rich and gave to the poor.

Lena had become so caught up in the story, she had almost forgotten she was trying to find out for her grandmother's sake. Now she wanted to know the truth for her own sake. She had come to love those two girls who had comforted each other through bad times. If she were honest, she had also fallen a little in love with Anton — not the Count as he was now, though he was certainly still a handsome man — but the young man from years ago who had made a silly mistake and had suffered for it.

No one could help who they fell in love with. As she thought that, she looked across at Greg, who was looking at her. He too was brave and honourable, leaving a relatively safe life in London to save the grandfather he adored. She glanced away, suddenly shy.

'What happened next?' Selena Garibaldi asked the Count. 'How did you and your wife come to fall in love after such a difficult start? What happened to the maid, Polly? And how did my grandfather help to save the Countess?'

Before the Count could respond, he was interrupted by a low hum coming from outside. The noise became louder, as whatever it was came closer to the bus and crowds of people walking outside.

Ivan slammed the breaks on. 'Get down!' he cried to everyone.

They all scrambled to the floor. Lena slid onto the floor, dragging Reuben after her. Sister Dominique covered Rachel's body with hers. The Count did the same with Selena and her child.

Outside people were diving off into the ditch at the side of the road, as planes flew overhead and started to drop bombs on the road, breaking it up so that the way was impassable by vehicle. Up in front, one vehicle flew into the air, and rolled over and over before landing in a field, where it exploded into flames.

'Oh, those poor souls!' Sister Dominique said, crossing herself and muttering an incantation. Outside, the planes were turning around, ready to make another run.

'We have to get off the bus now,' Greg shouted above the hum. 'They don't know which vehicle we're in, so they're going to hit them all.'

'We've put people in danger,' the Count said.

'We all chose to be here on this journey,' Selena Garibaldi said. 'We are all Cariastan. We stick together.'

Greg opened the door and people rushed off the bus with even more speed than they had boarded it, running into the ditch and the fields beyond, where it was too dark for them to be seen. Lena carried Reuben off, aided by someone who held up the oxygen tank. It was only when she was lying in the field that she remembered. 'The spare oxygen,' she said, standing up and starting to run towards the bus. She felt a force knock her down onto her stomach. 'Ooft! I have to get it.'

'No,' Greg's voice said in her ear. She could feel his weight on her back, and when she tried to move, he refused to budge. 'Stay down,' he hissed. At that moment one of the planes came around and peppered the bus with bombs. It exploded in a ball of fire. The noise was deafening, which made the deadly silence afterwards, when the planes turned to make another run, even more harrowing. 'I'm sorry, Lena, but you would have died in those flames if I hadn't stopped you.'

'I know,' she said, tears pricking her eyes.

She could not remember ever knowing such fear. She could barely breathe and not just because Greg had her pinned down. She had lived in a world where the people she loved had kept her safe from any darkness. Her grandmother's and parents' love had enveloped her in a protective shield. That had stripped away, to show her how much terror there was in the world. How much terror was to come, when the war finally began. The scenes they were witnessing now would be played out all over the world and on an even bigger scale. These good people were among the first to suffer its effects. It was almost too much to bear.

Greg moved to the side of her and stroked her hair back out of her eyes. 'I'm sorry for dragging you into this,' he whispered.

'I am terrified and distressed,' she

admitted. 'But I am not sorry that I came with you. I've been cosseted too long. Like many people, I have even thought that war might be rather exciting. I needed to see this, to understand the horrors we are facing. Is everyone alright?'

Greg looked around. 'Grandfather?'

'Yes, we all safe,' the Count said from somewhere among the wheat.

Sister Dominique murmured, 'Yes, we are well,' but she sounded shaken.

Lena, afraid of standing up and making a target of herself, crawled across to Reuben, where Rachel had joined him. She was holding onto her brother tight. 'Are you alright, my darlings?' she asked.

'Yes,' Reuben nodded. Rachel also nodded, her bravado having all but disappeared. Reuben's breathing was worse than ever, and she did not know how they were going to manage with only one oxygen tank.

At that moment, they had other concerns, and that involved staying alive long enough to find another oxygen supply. The planes were coming back, and this time appeared to be shooting in all directions, not just on the vehicles on the road. Any one of the hundreds of people hiding among the wheat could be hurt indiscriminately. The pilots just did not care who they hurt.

'Keep down,' Greg ordered from the distance.

Suddenly, there was the sound of more planes coming. Everyone held their breath, sure that they could not survive such an onslaught. Except the other planes were not firing at them. They were firing at the German planes, drawing them into a skirmish far away into the fields, where no one was hiding. Slowly, but surely, German planes started to fall.

'It's the King's Air Corps!' Ivan called. 'I'll bet he's flying one of them! They say he is an ace pilot!'

'God bless him,' said Sister Dominique.

The skirmish seemed to last an age, and all they could do was watch, as the

King's planes knocked one after another of the German planes out of the air. Finally, the German planes were all gone from the sky, and the Cariastan planes turned for home.

Everyone stood up, somewhat shakily. 'We have a long walk,' said Greg.

'Greg, I don't know . . . ' Lena started to say.

'I can do it,' said Reuben. 'I can, I promise.'

She took his hand on one side, and Rachel's on the other. She had come to love these children in the short time she had known them. Their safety was paramount. 'You're both so brave,' she said. 'I'm very proud of you.'

They all went back onto the road, or what parts of it were passable, and began the long walk south. The people who had been on the bus with them spread out, and Lena wondered if they had all survived. She had wanted to go and look, but Greg said they had to move on quickly in case the Germans sent more planes.

'They could be coming off the North African coast,' he said. 'It's possible they may send more. I'm sorry, Lena, but we can't risk anymore delays.'

The others became the echoes of that night, people they had known so briefly, but who they would not forget in a hurry.

She was relieved to see Selena Garibaldi walking up ahead with her child. They at least, were safe. As if realising she was being watched, Selena turned and then slowed her pace while they caught up with her. In a short time, she had become one of their group. These, Lena thought, were the sort of brief, but deep, connections one made in a time of strife.

'Tell us more about Polly and Clara,' Rachel said to the Count, after about ten minutes of silent walking. Her little hand still trembled in Lena's. 'Please.'

21

1890

Polly made her way to the hotel where the Shirebrooks were staying. The Scheherazade was a large, airy building of yellow sandstone in the centre of Caria's business quarter, with a shaded garden area which had tables and chairs, and a large foyer, with amber marble pillars, a high glass domed ceiling, and a magnificent staircase leading to a mezzanine floor where a string quartet played a local folk song and tourists enjoyed an English style afternoon tea or, for the more adventurous, the strong coffee and honey sweet Baklava favoured by the Cariastan locals.

'There she is,' she heard a voice say. 'Polly, up here, lass!'

She followed the sound up to the mezzanine and saw Eddie and Violet waving at her. She made her way up to them, smiling with genuine pleasure at seeing them again. Though she had hesitated at the idea of wearing one of Clara's old dresses, she had not wanted to enter the hotel in her maid's uniform. She wore a simple dress, covered in forget-me-nots, and a straw bonnet with a wide ribbon that matched the dress.

Eddie and Violet were sitting at a table near to the window, with their two lively children, Charity and Joshua, who were covered in sticky Baklava.

Violet kissed Polly on the cheek. 'You do look pretty,' she said, when Polly was seated and tea had been ordered. 'How is Anton?'

'He's much better, thank you,' Polly said, stiffly. She did not want to have to explain everything to them. She had not sorted it all out in her own head yet.

'We had hoped to see him,' said Eddie, as if fishing for more information. 'We never got to meet him properly on the boat.'

'He's very busy,' Polly said. 'With the Ambassador.' It was only half a lie. The

Ambassador had been taking part in the preparations for the wedding. It seemed that Anton and Clara's marriage was politically strategic. An alliance between Cariastan nobility and a British family was needed to strengthen ties between the two countries.

'And how is your friend, Miss Clara?' Violet asked. 'Is she looking forward to her wedding?'

'Actually, that's why I am glad we met today. Are you still looking for a mother's help?'

'We are indeed,' said Eddie. 'Do you know anyone, lass?'

'Yes, me.'

'What?' Eddie and Violet said together.

'It would only be temporary, until you return to England. Then I can go back to my old place. But I want to go home.' Polly felt the tears prick the back of her eyes and prayed she could keep her calm. 'It's not really the place for me, Cariastan.'

Eddie and Violet looked at her then at each other. They were sometimes brash, and did not always speak tactfully, yet even they understood at that moment that it was best not to press for information. 'The job is yours as soon as you want to start, isn't that right, Vi?' Eddie said.

'Yes. Oh yes. Charity and Joshua love you and we think of you as one of the family. You'll be staying with Miss Clara for the wedding, though?'

Polly shook her head. 'No. In fact, the sooner I can start with you, the better. Today even.' She laughed, trying to make light of it, but there was no light in her heart. She knew Eddie and Violet were good people, who she was lucky to call friends. But her heart would remain in Cariastan and she did not think that would ever change.

'Start tomorrow,' Eddie said. 'We're going sightseeing up at that White Peak and we'll need the help to keep these two from falling off it.'

'Don't go wearing servant clothes, either,' Violet said, as if guessing what Polly was going to ask next. 'Wear what you're wearing now. You look so pretty. Besides, you're my helper, not my servant.'

They spent the next half hour discussing salaries and what the itinerary was for the next day. By the end of it, Polly began to feel hopeful. She would still be working, but she also had a taste of freedom. Clara could never have taken her on outings. It was not the done thing in England. As a mother's help, even if only for a short time, she would be treated on par with the family. She left them to return to the ambassador's villa.

Feeling suddenly emboldened, she entered via the front door. As the butler just let her in without comment, she could only assume that he did not recognise her. She was about to go upstairs when her name was called.

'Polly?' It was Anton. He stood at the door to his study. 'I would like to speak to you for a moment, please?'

As she did not want to cause a scene with the butler listening in, she could only obey. She followed him into the study and he closed the door. It said everything about how he viewed her. He and Clara had not been able to meet without a chaperone, yet he did not even consider Polly's reputation as he ordered her into the study.

'I'm sorry there is no one to chaperone us,' he said, cutting into her exact thoughts in a way that was unnerving. 'Please do not take it as a poor measure of my respect for you. Be assured that I hold you in the highest esteem. It is just that what I have to say can only be said in private. For your sake, not mine.'

'Oh?' Polly said. He gestured to an armchair near to the fireplace, but she shook her head. 'I prefer to stand.' She felt stronger and more in control that way. He may be a Count, but she would not let him lord it over her. Her dignity was all she had left. 'What about all the times we were alone on the ship? Did my esteem not matter then?'

He had no answer for that and moved to change the subject. 'I wanted you to know that I spoke to Mrs Lovett yesterday.'

'I see. If you're going to dismiss me, there is no need. I have already found employment. I will be leaving tomorrow.'

'Tomorrow?' He shook his head, clearly aghast at the news. 'I had no idea. But why? You have done nothing wrong.'

'We both know that's not true. I told my best friend's husband that I was in love with him. I think she has a right to feel angry, don't you?'

'Polly, if there is any fault then it is mine alone. Your behaviour has been impeccable, all along. I told Clara that. It is also the reason I spoke to Mrs Lovett yesterday. I told her that I do not care how servants have been treated in other homes in which she has stayed, but none in Cariastan will ever be spoken to the way she spoke to you yesterday. I also told her that your family history was none of her business. She had no right to shame you in that way.'

'Even though it was true.'

'Especially because it was true. You

are not responsible for any choices your mother may or may not have made. Besides, actresses are not as vilified here as they are in your country. In fact, the ambassador's late wife was an actress before their marriage and she was a woman of great honour.'

'Is that all you wanted to say?' she asked. It tore at her that he was being so reasonable and kind. It would have been easier if he had joined in the shaming of her. It would help if he did not hold her in such esteem, then she could hate him and her life would be much easier.

'No. I wanted to apologise for what she said. You should not have had to face that. I also wanted to apologise for my behaviour. I never meant for things to turn out the way they did. I thought it was a bit of fun. That I would eventually throw off my disguise and that Clara would be amused. It was foolish of me. As I told her, you happened. Even then I denied my feelings. Even as I followed you onto the *Caria*, I told myself I was only looking after my future wife's best friend, and that she would be happy that I did that. My feelings for you . . .'

'Please don't.' Polly held up her hand. 'It is hard enough as it is. Don't you see?'

'For me too.'

'No, not for you. You will have Clara and if you give yourself time, you will love her. You can do nothing else but love her, unless you have no common sense whatsoever. I will make it easier for you both by leaving. To give you a chance. But I warn you,' she said, looking him straight in the eye. 'If I ever find out you have hurt or shamed her in any way, I will come back and deal with you myself.'

Anton's lips curled into a wry smile. 'I am sure you and she were twins separated at birth, for you both say the same thing to me.'

'We were friends before you came along. One day, God willing, we will be friends again.'

She doubted it very much, because he would always be there, between them. Soon, he and Clara would be married, and know an intimacy that tore Polly in two to consider.

'And you and I?' he asked. She saw her heartbreak reflected in his eyes. Even though what they felt for each other was wrong, it was impossible to turn those feelings off.

'We can be nothing to each other.'

'I know this,' he said. 'I just needed to hear you say it.'

'Goodbye, Anton.'

'Goodbye, Polly.'

For the second time that week, she had to leave behind someone she loved. She longed for the warmth of Bessie's kitchen, and the familiarity of Derwent Priory, even with the Harringtons as master and mistress. Somehow, their stinginess and mean-mindedness had not touched the staff quarters. With Bessie, Mrs Turner and Mrs Jenkins at the helm, staff were protected. Polly longed for that protection again. Protection from all the pain she had endured in losing Clara's friendship and the possibility of a lifelong love with Anton.

As she went to her room to hide and to cry again, she told herself that girls like her were not allowed epic love affairs with handsome members of the nobility. They were supposed to marry the plain but solidly reliable farmers' or butchers' boys, like poor Harriet Smith in Jane Austen's *Emma*. A few months ago, she might have been content with that. She did not see herself as being above them or even too good for them. Far from it. But Anton had showed her a world of possibilities, then stripped that world away from her. It would be difficult to go back to what she had been, knowing how different things could be. As a servant she had neither expected nor wanted a grand love in her life. Now she had tasted that, she wished she could go back to the time she did not know how that love felt, to put an end to the pain in her heart.

She remembered being on the boat, dancing with Anton, the warmth of his hand searing through the thin satin of her dress, arousing her in ways she had never known possible. She had gone to bed with the imprint of his hands tormenting her dreams, imagining how it would feel if her dress and corset were not in the way. Now she thought about how those hands would one day be touching her dearest friend and she shivered and pushed the thought aside as being sinful and wrong. If she went down that route of remembering his touch, she might end up hating them both, and she did not want that.

Polly had barely reached her room for her much-needed cry when a footman caught up with her and said that the ambassador wished to see her in the drawing room.

She turned heel and began her descent to the first floor, where the drawing room spread all across the front of the villa, with three sets of French doors leading out onto a veranda.

'Miss Smith,' said the ambassador, bowing slightly. 'I am sorry to have bothered you.' His cheeks were flushed, and he kept looking at his feet, as if whatever was down there was preferable to what he was facing. 'This is very difficult. Yes, very difficult. Mrs Lovett said that Miss Clara did not want to have to do this, and she herself — Mrs Lovett that is — felt that things between you and her were left on an awkward footing yesterday. Something for which she takes the blame. She said she spoke irrationally only due to her fondness for Miss Clara.' He looked up. 'Oh, please, be seated. You must think me very rude.' He gestured to a chaise longue.

Polly sat down, wondering what was going to come next. She wondered whether Mrs Lovett had told the ambassador exactly what had been said, after Anton's censure.

She did not let herself be drawn on Mrs Lovett. Quite simply she hated the simpering fool. She also recognised that this was because it was easier to direct her hate and anger towards the chaperone than to blame Clara and Anton for the recent events.

'What is it, Ambassador?' Polly said,

kindly. Though they had not spent time together, she had no reason to be angry with him. He seemed like a decent man, caught up in a drama not of his making.

'I have been tasked with giving you your ticket home,' the ambassador said. 'Miss Clara has also included some money for incidentals.'

He passed Polly a thick wad of papers. She opened them to see a ticket for First Class passage on the *Dominique*, which would leave the following day, and some cash. It was more than Polly normally earned in a year. There was also a booking for a hotel room for several nights until the ship left. She looked for a note, but was disappointed to find none.

'She wanted you to be as comfortable returning to England as you were when you left,' the Ambassador said. 'As a way of thanking you for your devoted service.' He was every bit the diplomat.

Polly folded the papers back up and stood up, handing them back to the Ambassador. 'Thank you,' she said, 'but I have made other arrangements.

Tomorrow I take up another post with a British family, and I will travel back with them. They have arranged for me to have a room at the hotel where they are staying.'

'Oh, I see.' The ambassador looked at her with even more kindness than before. 'That was a very wise move, I think, Miss Smith.'

'Of course, if you would prefer me to leave the villa today, I can do so, but I will pay for my own hotel.' She still had a few pounds left from the money that Anton had given her. Although part of her hated to use it, because she had already spent some of it, it did not feel as bad as taking money from Clara now, when things between them were so difficult.

'Miss Smith, may I say that you have behaved impeccably these past few days, despite the ... er ... difficult circumstances. I am not unaware of what has happened. It was something I feared when the Count took such an interest in your welfare. What I am saying is that, as this is my home, you are more than welcome to remain as a guest until you take up your new post tomorrow. In fact, as you will be my guest, I will have your things moved to a more suitable room, as a mark of my respect for you.'

'Thank you, Ambassador, but that is not necessary. I don't mind sleeping in the servants' quarters. That is my role in life, after all.'

And until now she had not cared, but suddenly she felt constrained by her class and status. If only she was a rich girl . . . but she pushed the thought aside. That way only lay madness.

'Yes. Yes, I suppose that is correct. One day, we can only hope that such class distinctions do not matter. They certainly don't to me. My late wife was an actress, you know?'

So, he had known what Mrs Lovett had said to her. 'I had heard,' Polly said. 'I'm sorry I did not meet her.'

'Her Lady Macbeth was a sight to behold,' he said. 'Terrifying, even! Yet, in reality she was the gentlest, noblest woman I have ever known. What I am saying is that you do not have to let others define you, or your mother. I have no doubt you have it within you to be whatever you want to be.'

'Unfortunately,' said Polly with a sad smile. 'The rest of the world has not yet caught up with either of us.'

'It will,' said the ambassador. 'Maybe not in my lifetime, but it will.'

Polly left him and was finally able to return to her room and pack.

She spent the rest of the day out of the way of everyone. She had no duties to perform. At dinner time, Fatima knocked on her door, with a tray of delicious food. Polly had been lying on the bed, thinking about her future, yet found she could not think past the next day.

'We will miss you,' she said to Polly. 'We will miss your red hair and your loud laughter.'

'Thank you, Fatima. I wish we'd had more time to become friends.'

'It is not the length of a friendship that matters,' said Fatima. 'It is the quality. If you need anything while you are still in

Cariastan, you only have to ask us.'

Polly was not sure if it was culturally correct, but she hugged Fatima anyway. The woman seemed taken aback, then she smiled. 'Mad Englishwomen,' she laughed. 'Always they seem reserved, then their feelings burst forth.'

After Fatima left, Polly ate what she could, then she tried to sleep, but sleep would not come.

She left the villa in the early morning, so she could slip away before anyone woke up. At the gates, she turned back for one last look and saw them both watching her — Clara in one window and Anton in another.

Her heart split in two, with one half going to her former best friend and the other to the man she loved. Once again, she was saying goodbye to all that she had known. Even though Anton had not been in her life long, she had almost forgotten what it was like before him.

She raised her hand in an insubstantial wave, then was gone, lost in the morning mist.

22

'I think they should have both gone after her,' said Rachel. 'They're not real friends if they let her just go like that.' Then, as if remembering who she was with, she said, 'Sorry, Count, but . . . well . . . she was awfully nice, and you both just let her go away.'

They had walked a couple of miles. Somewhere along the way, they had found an abandoned cart, and sat Reuben on it. They took it in turns to push him. It was hard going, over the rough ground, but he was exhausted from walking.

'So, that was what happened to her,' Lena said. 'She just went to work for the Shirebrooks and returned to England? Why could you not have just told me that, Greg?' She shook her head. 'It doesn't make sense. If she had come home, like she said, she would have contacted my nana.'

Reuben spoke up. It was one of the rare occasions he did speak. He usually let his sister do all the talking for him. He pulled the mask off.

'How do you know all this stuff about what Polly was thinking and feeling?' he asked the Count. 'How do you know her heart broke in two? If she went away, how do you know about her seeing the Ambassador?'

Lena was relieved to see that hearing the story had helped him breathe more easily. It had calmed him down and eased his stress.

Sister Dominique was pushing him. Like everyone else, she had listened intently to the story, smiling occasionally and looking pensive during other parts. Lena somehow got the impression she knew some of it, although not all.

'The ambassador told me about it,' said the Count, smiling.

'I hadn't thought of that.' Reuben lay back.

'The rest I am imagining from things I have heard since.'

'You didn't tell us about your wife's life being saved by Mr Garibaldi,' Rachel said, in accusing tones. 'You said you would.'

'I was building up to it, then you interrupted to tell me I was a bad friend to Polly Smith.' His shoulders were shaking slightly, as if he was holding in laughter. Lena thought that it seemed an odd way to behave, after admitting to breaking a young woman's heart.

'Oh, yes. Sorry.' Rachel looked abashed. 'But you did hurt her badly, which was a very rotten thing to do.'

'My heart was broken too,' the Count said.

'Yes, but now you love your wife, but poor Polly had no one.'

'It's called being a grown up,' Lena said, tousling Rachel's hair, playfully. 'It is possible to love more than one person in a lifetime. There are also different types of love. Like the love Polly had for her friend, compared to the love she had for the Count.'

'How are they different?'

'Well,' said Greg, grinning. 'That's something you'll have to find out when you're a grown up.' He winked at Lena and she could not help laughing.

'Maybe we should wait till I grow up,' she quipped.

'We're only a couple of miles from the airfield,' Greg said. 'We need to turn off at the next crossroads. Does anyone need to rest? Grandfather?'

'I would rather keep going. Sister Dominique? How is your leg?'

'There is a reason I am holding the cart,' she said with a gentle smile. 'I can go on for a while with young Reuben's help.'

Reuben smiled, looking proud to have been helping somehow.

Lena would have liked to have stopped. She had not slept for over twenty-four hours, and any adrenalin had long since drained, but if two elderly people could manage the rest of the walk, then she could keep going.

'Lena?' Greg said, touching her shoulder.

'I'm fine,' she said, with a wide, fixed smile.

'You can sleep on the plane,' he promised.

'What about you?'

'It's not a good idea for the pilot to take a nap.'

'Seriously, Greg, will you be able to do it?'

'My grandfather is a pilot, and so is Ivan. Either can take over.'

'That's a relief. Ivan is a good man.'

Ivan was walking up ahead with Selena Garibaldi. They had struck up a bit of a flirtation after Selena had revealed she was widowed. It was another example of the brief but intense connections that people made during difficult times. Where it would end, no one knew.

Lena wondered if that was the case with her feelings for Greg. They had known each other only a couple of days, yet if felt as if he had been in her life forever. When it was all over, they would no doubt go their separate ways, and eventually this would all be a vague memory.

'Gregori!' Ivan called, pointing towards the southern coast. 'That must be the *Caria* and the *Dominique*.'

Everyone looked up, and saw two ships out in the harbour. They were moving closer to the land. The word went up to all the refugees moving south and it energised them. The crowds began heading towards the coast rapidly, surging forward to reach the coast.

Only Greg and Lena's group held back, and Selena Garibaldi stayed with them, having become a part of their temporary family. They eventually reached the crossroads, leading to the airfield.

'Greg?' Lena said, stopping.

'Yes?'

'I'm thinking . . . will the ships have medical supplies?'

'Yes, they should be fully kitted out.'

She turned to him. 'Then I have to get Reuben onto one of them. We're not going to make it in the plane. His oxygen tank is nearly empty.'

'Lena, we don't have time to go by boat. I have to get my grandfather back immediately. It's of utmost importance. The truth is, he has a special mission for the King.'

'I guessed as much and I understand. I'm not asking you to come with me.'

'I'm not leaving my brother,' Rachel said, becoming tearful.

'No, of course not, darling,' Lena said, putting her arm around Rachel's shoulders. 'You come with us.'

'You don't know how long it's going to take to get back to England by boat,' Greg protested. 'The ships might have engines now but it still takes at least a week to get to England, and we don't know when this war will begin. You may not make it past the African coast. The Germans have already occupied parts of North Africa.'

'Isn't that the risk that everyone getting on the boats is going to take?' Lena pointed out.

'Yes, but they will be content to be set down anywhere safe in the region. You may not make it home at all until after the war has ended. I would never forgive myself if that happened.'

'Greg, I'm a grown woman. I make my own decisions. I chose to be here, now I choose this. I cannot risk Reuben on that flight.'

'Greg,' said Ivan, 'You take your grandfather and Sister Dominique to the airfield, and I will take Doctor Turner and the children to the coast and put them on the ship. Selena is going that way too.'

'If we don't hurry up, we're going to miss the boats,' Lena said.

Greg nodded. 'Yes, I understand what you're saying. I don't like it, but I understand you need to do it for Reuben's sake.'

He put his hand on her shoulders. 'I owe you dinner when you return.'

'You owe me lots of dinners,' she said, with a smile.

'Thank you for everything,' he said.

He leaned forward and kissed her on the cheek. For a moment his lips lingered there and she thought he might kiss her properly, but he drew back, perhaps mindful they had an audience. 'You'd better come and find me when you return, Doctor Lena Turner. Whenever that may be.'

'You can count on it.'

They all said goodbye at the crossroads. Lena found herself hugging the Count and Sister Dominique as if they were old friends she had known since childhood. There were tears and promises to keep in touch. They walked in their separate directions, waving for as long as they could, until they were too far apart to see each other clearly. Whether that was the distance or the tears, Lena did not know. 'Are you and Greg going to get married?' Rachel asked. 'I really think you should.'

Lena did not know whether to laugh or cry then.

She turned one last time, and thought she still saw Greg far away in the distance. Or perhaps it was just an echo . . .

23

The *Caria* sailed into Portsmouth Harbour on a sunny day in early September. The passengers, who had been packed in like sardines, welcomed the chance to get off and find their land legs again. Lena walked down the gangplank, holding Rachel's hand, and watching as stretcher bearers ahead carried Reuben. He had improved on the trip, the sea air and relevant calm helping him, but he still needed hospitalisation and a course of antibiotics to ensure he was finally free of the pneumonia.

Lena and Rachel climbed into the back of an ambulance with him and they were taken to a hospital in Portsmouth, where he was immediately put onto an antibiotic drip and given a more permanent supply of oxygen. Lena had arranged for Rachel to sleep in a bed on her brother's ward, telling the staff, 'She needs tending to as well. She's been through a traumatic time and the conditions on the ship were less than sanitary with so many people crammed onto it. Check her vitals every four hours and report to me.'

There was nothing really wrong with Rachel and Lena knew it was wrong to take up a bed that might be needed by others, but she understood that the little girl would never agree to being separated from her brother, and it helped Reuben to have her nearby. They had no one else.

A few days later, once they were settled in, and Lena had managed to get a few days proper rest in the hospital staff accommodation, she told them she was going to London. She had popped out that morning to buy some new clothes for herself and also some for the children, including pyjamas.

'I'll be back for you both,' she promised. Reuben had improved considerably and there was talk of discharging him within a couple of days. He would still need care and attention, but he could get that better in a settled home.

'It's alright if you don't,' Rachel said, sadly. 'People never come back when they promise to.'

'Do you want me to inform the authorities about them?' the matron asked. She was listening nearby. 'They'll need to be found a family.'

'They're going to stay with me,' Lena said.

'Doctor Turner, I don't think . . . '

'If you were going to say you don't think they should go to absolute strangers after a stressful and unsettling journey, I absolutely agree with you. I'm all they know and I won't abandon them.'

The matron gave her a sharp look and then left the ward.

'Can we stay with you?' Rachel asked. 'Do you mean it?'

'Do you want to?' It occurred to her that she should have asked them first what they wanted.

'Oh, we do, don't we, Reuben?'

Reuben nodded eagerly.

'I mean it then,' she said, feeling some relief now she had made the decision properly. 'I have to be honest with you, I'm not sure if they'll let me keep you. I don't know what the rules are. But I will do everything in my power to make it happen.'

'And Greg?' Reuben said. 'Will he be there? I do wish he had given me a ride in his plane.'

'Well, that's up to him,' said Lena, blushing. He may not want any part in the life she had decided to have with the children. He had only known them a couple of days, whereas Lena had spent over a week in confinement with them on the ship and had come to love them as if they were her own flesh and blood. Losing whatever connection she might have with him was a risk she was prepared to take to make sure they had a permanent home in the future.

'Will we call you mummy?' Rachel asked.

'Only if you want to.'

'Alright, Mummy,' said Reuben, smiling through his mask. Lena hugged them both.

'Remember that I love you and I will be back for you,' she said. 'You'll be safe here for now.'

'Matron doesn't like us,' Rachel said.

'She's not a bad person,' Lena said. 'She just has her own way of doing things. And she's very busy, so be kind to her.'

'Do we have to not be Jews anymore?' Rachel asked. 'The last family who were going to take us refused because we said we didn't want to become Catholics.'

'You can be anything you want to be,' said Lena. 'I don't know much about Judaism, but I will learn everything I can to help you.'

She felt tearful as she left them, already feeling that she was a bad mother. But she also wanted to see Greg and his family to make sure they were all safe. She took the train to London and stopped off at the Cariastan Embassy.

'I'm sorry, Doctor Turner,' a young attaché told her, 'But Mr Di Luca has already travelled north with his family.'

'Oh, I see. North?'

'Yes, to Scarborough. He did leave

you a note. Wait there a moment.' The attaché disappeared into the office, then returned with a thick envelope.

Lena took it from him then went to nearby park where she sat down and opened the envelope. A loose note fell out, and it said: *Come to your grandmother's as soon as you can. I've included some light reading for the train. Bring the children if they're still with you. Greg xxx*

As well as Greg's note, there was a longer handwritten letter, then several typed pages. She glanced at the letter and then saw the signature at the bottom. Her heart flipped over.

Dear Doctor Turner,

I can only apologise that it has taken this long to be able to tell you the truth about what happened to me. I know you have heard much of the story, if not all of it, albeit in fits and starts.

Gregori speaks all the time of your courage and compassion. He speaks all the time of you!

I apologise for not being there to meet you on your return from Cariastan. I have

decided to travel north to see your grandmother for myself, and set her mind at rest,
as I believe, knowing of your love for her,
that you would want this more than anything. It is my way of thanking you for your
service to our country.

I hope the pages that I have prepared for
you will fill in the final part of my story, and
that knowing all the facts at last, you will
forgive me for my subterfuge.

Yours faithfully,
Polly Smith

24

Clara sat on at a table in the inner courtyard of the convent, twirling her parasol
slowly and allowing the sun to warm her
face. It was the most peaceful she had
felt since her arrival in Cariastan. Here
she could be herself and she did not have
to pretend.

'It is very nice,' said Mrs Lovett. 'Very
holy, if you know what I mean.'

Clara smiled kindly, but wished that
her chaperone was not there. Over the
past few days there had not been a silence
that the good lady had not thought she
should fill. It was as if she was nervous
about something.

'I think you're more stressed about
my wedding than I am,' Clara had said
to her the day before.

'I only want to know I have done my
duty to your aunt and uncle,' Mrs Lovett

said.

'Have no fear, Mrs Lovett. I'll let my aunt and uncle know that you have behaved impeccably.' She was not aware of what had been said to Polly.

They had set out for the convent soon after breakfast that morning, so as to reach it before the sun was too high in the sky. They took a carriage most of the way, then had to walk the rest of the narrow pathway on foot.

Sister Marie-Claire joined them with glasses of cold, sweet lemonade. 'Made from our own lemons,' she told them, as she put the tray on the table. 'I find it tastes better with a dash of port, but it's too early in the day, even for me.'

'You are a one,' Mrs Lovett said, laughing in brittle tones. 'She does tease, doesn't she, Miss Clara?'

'I assure you she doesn't,' said Clara smiling. 'She drank me under the table on the voyage over. I love it here,' she said to Sister Marie-Claire. 'I wish I could stay.'

'There's nothing to stop you, child,'

said Marie Claire. 'You don't have to do anything you don't want to.'

'I have made a promise. A legal and binding promise,' Clara explained. 'I don't think taking up the veil would be in keeping with that promise. Besides, I only want to run away because things are so difficult at the moment.'

'Tell me more about what happened. If you want to.' The sister glanced at Mrs Lovett.

'I don't think Mrs Lovett is unaware of events,' Clara said.

She filled Sister Marie Claire in on everything that had happened since they last met, up to the day she watched Polly leave in the early hours.

'It's always very sad to lose a servant,' Mrs Lovett said, before anyone else spoke. 'But there are good ladies maids everywhere, isn't that right, Sister?'

'I gather from what Miss Clara has told me about young Polly that they were great friends,' the sister said.

'With a maid? I know Miss Clara has a kind and charitable heart and that is all

it ever was. Showing kindness to someone less fortunate than herself. It was
pity that the girl betrayed her.'

Clara pursed her lips. She did not
appreciate hearing Mrs Lovett describ-
ing her friendship with Polly as that of a
lady bountiful with someone to be pitied.
'There was nothing pitiable about Polly,'
she said, in controlled tones. 'She was a
very capable and clever person. And she
did not betray me.'

'Of course,' said Mrs Lovett. 'I don't
say she wasn't a good girl. Within her
own limitations.'

Clara stood up and went to walk
around the courtyard. She pressed her
lips together, fighting back to the urge
to lay into Mrs Lovett. Her parasol spun
with the effort of keeping her emotions
in check.

'No, you stay there,' she heard the Sister say to her chaperone. 'Let me deal
with this.'

'If you prefer good Sister. I fear I
always say the wrong thing. I only mean
to be kind.'

'You do? Oh, you do.'

Clara recognised the wry tone in the sister's voice, even if it went over Mrs Lovett's head. She stopped to look at a frieze of the Garden of Eden.

'You're hurt, child,' the sister murmured when she drew close to her.

'She was my best friend and I've lost her. It wasn't her fault, despite what Mrs Lovett says. My future husband and I have treated her appallingly. I am not proud of my behaviour.'

'I understand.'

'But I have to get married. I have to break free from my aunt and uncle. The only way I can do that is to release my fortune. Otherwise, I would have to wait another four and a half years. I cannot bear that house any longer. Forgive me my selfishness. I don't deserve a friend like Polly and I don't deserve your sympathy.'

'I can hardly censure you, when you so readily insist on self-flagellation. What of the Count? Do you think you will ever fall in love with him?'

Clara shook her head. 'I barely know him. From what I do know, I believe him to be a good, honourable man. He did a foolish thing, in pretending to be a valet, but he did not behave wickedly, either to me or to Polly. I believe he loves her very much. Personally speaking, I don't care about that. At least for now. But in the future that is going to matter, when we become . . .' Clara paused, blushing. 'Intimate. It will be her he dreams of in those moments, not me. My heart may not be hurt, but I don't know if my pride can take spending my life with a man who prefers the company of another. The worst of it is that I will feel as if I am betraying her too. because of the love they hold for each other. It feels as if she is already his wife, and I will be the mistress.'

'That will not be true when you are married in the eyes of God.'

'Forgive me for saying this, Sister Marie-Claire, but I don't think God has much say in this matter. Not when it comes to feelings. Morally we may do the right thing, legally we most certainly are carrying out our parents' wishes, but emotionally we are all being untrue to ourselves. And now you will think me awful for spouting such blasphemy. I apologise if I have offended you.'

'My dear child, do you think I have reached the age I am without sometimes railing against God? Without questioning how He can allow bad things to happen to good people while the wicked thrive? The Ten Commandments are a good set of tenets by which to live one's life, it is true. But that does not mean that we won't sometimes find it hard to keep them. If a man's family is starving, is it so wrong for him to steal? The bible says yes, but his children's hungry bellies say no. The man is doing what he must. In the end, all we can be is true to ourselves. Remember that your promise to your future husband was made long before he met your friend, so when you go to him as his wife, you are not betraying anyone.'

Clara nodded. 'I know this is true.'

She had told herself that too. 'But, I still cannot take it to heart.'

'And at least you don't have to live with the fact that they betrayed you. I think, from what you have told me, they have both acted honourably.'

'I know that too. But I'm afraid I may not have, sending her away. She sent me a letter this morning and I could not even bring myself to read it,' Clara told her.

'You will find the right moment and I am sure you will be glad of the comfort it brings you.'

'Miss Clara?' Mrs Lovett cooed from the other side of the garden. 'If we're to visit the White Peak . . . '

Clara sighed. 'Oh, I had forgotten about that.'

'What is this about the White Peak?' asked the Sister.

'Mrs Lovett wants to go and see it, but I have come to believe it's where my parents died. Where many others have died too. I don't know if I want to go there. It's an evil place.'

'It is a place, like any other,' said Sister Marie Claire. 'There are no evil places. Only the evil that men do in those places.'

'Do you think I should go?'

'Oh no. Certainly not. I can't even comprehend why she would think you would want to go there. It's rather callous of her, if you ask me.'

Clara laughed. 'I want to tell you how much I have appreciated your kindness and honesty. I hope you will let me come to visit sometimes, once I am settled in my own home.'

'You are welcome here any time, child. I hope I shall visit you too. I hear the Count's home in the south is beautiful.'

'Yes, oh yes, please do. I will need a friend.'

Clara left the convent feeling far more at peace than when she had arrived. She had a friend, and that meant a lot in a strange land. She and Mrs Lovett were shown out and they heard the door lock behind them, yet she had the feeling of being watched as they walked away.

'I think we should just go back,' Clara

said, making a start to walk down the hill, back towards the city.

As she did, she saw people walking up the hill. There was a lone man, heading up the hill as if on some errand. Behind him was a family group of four, with a fifth person following along behind them. From a distance it was the dress she recognised first. A blue floral sundress, with a matching straw bonnet, that she used to own.

It was Polly and they were heading for the convent.

Clara could not get away without passing them, yet she did not want to ruin the calm she had found by having to face Polly. She could not deal with her yet. It was the reason she had sent her away.

'We'd best go to the White Peak then,' she said to Mrs Lovett, heading for the corner of the convent and the pathway that led higher up the hill.

She did not know if she only imagined hearing Polly shout, 'Clara, wait! Stop!' or if she had simply wished her friend would speak to her. She ignored the voice, whether in her head or otherwise, and kept on walking.

25

Polly called up the hill. 'Clara, wait! Stop!' She turned to her companions. 'Eddie, Violet! She's going up the hill with the Lovett woman and that man! We have to stop her.'

Picking up her petticoats, Polly sprinted ahead. As she ran, she shouted over her shoulder, 'Call at the convent. Tell them everything. Tell them to get help!'

It was only the day before that Polly began to piece together the truth, all because of something that occurred at the hotel. All the little accidents had been forgotten in light of the human drama playing out between three people. Distance had given her a chance to think more about the events leading up to their arrival in Cariastan. The gargoyle that almost landed on her. Anton's apparent food poisoning.

Then, while she was sitting in the hotel

foyer, waiting for Eddie, Violet and the children to join her, she looked up and saw a man entering the foyer. She knew his face, but at first could not place it. Then he looked straight at her, and she had that feeling of being assaulted again. The same one she felt on the night the boat's crew had let a lone man onto the ship. The same one she had felt seeing a strange porter going into Anton's cabin. It was him, and he was looking at her. He tried to pretend otherwise. To look around as if he was looking for someone in particular, but she had no illusions that she had already been found.

He turned on his heels and left. That was when things started to fall into place for Polly. All the attempts on hers and Anton's life. The attempt on her life was to stop her travelling with Clara, so that she had no one on her side other than their friend, Mrs Lovett. The attempt on Anton's life had been to stop him from marrying Clara. She had also heard rumours in the kitchens at the Priory that Clara's mother and father had not died in an accident. It was something she never spoke of with her friend, for fear of causing her pain.

In that moment, Polly came to believe that everything came back to Cariastan, and what had happened there some twenty years before.

There were only two people who would benefit from Clara and her parent's deaths and that was her aunt and uncle. Clara's mother and father dying left the Harringtons nominally in charge of Clara's inheritance, most of which her mother had the foresight to tie up in a trust fund that would only be released in its entirety when she married or reached the age of twenty-five. If Clara died, without a husband and leaving no issue, the Harringtons were her only beneficiaries. What better than to have it all happen hundreds of miles from Britain, where they could not be suspected of anything? First Clara's mother and father, then Clara herself!

'They tried to stop me coming,' she explained to Eddie and Violet when she got them alone in their room. 'They either meant to injure me, or to kill me. No one would have asked questions about my death. I'm nobody. It's why Mrs Harrington called me to the garden room. She knew I had to go via the outer door. They wanted to isolate Clara. When that failed, they somehow managed to get someone onto the *Caria* to poison Anton. That porter that I saw. The man with the look that could kill. He was just in the hotel. Meanwhile, I believe Mrs Lovett was trying to kill Clara on the *Dominique*. There was talk among the Ambassador's staff about a lifeboat coming off its moorings. They said it was an accident, but I bet it wasn't.'

She could tell by Eddie and Violet's expressions that they thought she had gone a bit mad. 'I know it sounds impossible, but I honestly believe she's in danger until she marries. I have to write to her. To warn her. I can't let Lovett see it. I know, I'll send it via Fatima and ask her to pass it on.'

'Listen, duck,' said Violet, gently.

'We know you've had a terrible time of it, with falling in love with your best friend's man and all that, but things like this don't happen to nice young English ladies. Or to nice young English ladies' maids for that matter.'

'If I am imagining it all, everyone can have a good laugh at my expense, but it won't matter because at least Clara will be safe and alive. Anton will be safe and alive. That's all I care about. They can lock me up as a madwoman if they want, as long as they get this message.'

Polly sat down and wrote a long letter, detailing all her concerns about the dangers facing Clara and Anton. When she had finished and read it back, it sounded ridiculous, even to her and she almost did not send it. Fear of what would happen if she was right, and yet did nothing, overtook any concerns she had about appearing foolish. She sent it with a messenger boy to the Ambassador's residence late in the evening.

She had half expected, or perhaps only hoped, to hear back almost immediately, but when the next morning came and with it no reply, she had no choice but to join Eddie and Violet on their walk.

She was grateful for their patience, because so far, she had done nothing to recommend herself as a mother's help. She had only come across as hysterical and dramatic. She vowed to make up for it, and began by concentrating all her efforts on the children and in giving Violet a break.

They were halfway up the hill to the convent when the man passed them. The same man who had been on the *Caria* and who had come to the hotel to look at Polly. Then she had seen Clara going towards White Peak with Mrs Lovett and had immediately forgotten the duties for which she was paid.

She picked up her skirts and ran like hell!

Her years of service had kept her fit, but not quite fit enough for a hill that steep, where the air grew thinner as she neared the top. A couple of times she had to stop, because of a stitch in her side, and because the air would not fill her lungs to capacity, but panic urged her on. What if she did not get there in time?

As she reached the summit, she saw that it flattened out, and that there was a low barrier on the steepest side, where the land fell away, to the vineyards in the foothills. Near the barrier she could only see Mrs Lovett and the man, who appeared to be trying to lift something off the barrier. With mounting horror, Polly realised that the something was Clara's fingertips.

'No!' she screamed, rushing the man in a rugby tackle. He made an 'ooft' sound and fell to the ground, hitting his head on the stone barrier as he did so.

Mrs Lovett dived at Polly. The two women fell to the ground, but Polly jumped straight back up to go to her friend.

'Polly!' Clara cried, clinging on. 'Help me!'

The drop below her made Polly dizzy, but she could not let Clara down.

'Get off her!' Mrs Lovett caught Polly by the hair, and pulled her back before she could grab Clara's hand. 'You meddling little witch! You should have died in England. They said you'd be trouble if you stayed with her! Always sticking your nose in where it doesn't belong.'

'Did you kill her parents?' Polly asked, trying to extricate herself. Her scalp was on fire.

'Think you're going to get a confession out of me at the last minute? This is not a novel, dearie. Let's just say that there are lots of people like me in the world, willing to do what needs to be done for a price.'

She pushed Polly back so that she was half hanging over the barrier, the valley far below her. Nearby, Clara sobbed and clung on for dear life.

'You won't get away with it this time,' Polly said. Her back felt as though it was breaking, as Mrs Lovett pushed her backwards. 'You've been seen. I told them to send help.' She scratched at the woman's hands, which had caught her around her throat.

'I can tell them how you killed Miss Clara so you could have her fiancé for yourself, then you fell over after I intervened to try to stop you. It's a tragic story for the ages. You've played right into my hands.'

'Oh, I don't think you're that clever,' Polly said. But it was true that Polly had created a motive for killing Clara.

This only made her struggle harder to get free She kicked Mrs Lovett hard in the shins, causing her to fall back. But the woman was too strong for her. She dived at Polly and they both went over the barrier.

As if everything was in slow motion, Polly heard Mrs Lovett scream, as she passed her, the scream dying away as the woman's body hit the ground far below.

At the same time, Clara lost her grip and fell too. Polly, who had caught hold of the barrier, reached out, trying to catch her.

Finally, she snatched Clara's hand,

and tried to pull her up, but her own grip on the barrier was not strong enough to take the weight of two people, and they fell together . . .

26

'Clara? Clara, are you awake?' What Polly really wanted to ask was 'Are you alive?'

She clung to the narrow ledge, where Clara had landed next to her. They were two thirds of the way down the cliff, closer to the bottom than the top. The ledge had broken their fall. Polly was relieved it had broken nothing else. At least of hers. But she had scratches and bruises everywhere. Her right elbow was red raw from where the fabric and skin had been scraped off. Her bonnet had been ripped off during the fight, leaving her no respite from the blazing sun.

She looked around for a means of getting down, but there was nothing. The cliff was a sheer drop, with only a few ledges here and there. There was nothing she could cling on to.

'Clara?'

'Polly . . .' Clara opened her blue eyes

and tried to sit up, then cried out. 'Polly, I think my leg is broken.' Tears filled her eyes, and she breathed with difficulty, due to the intense pain.

'It's alright. Eddie and Violet will get help.'

'Eddie and Violet? Oh, your new employers. What about Mrs Lovett?' Clara said, looking down.

'I don't think she can have survived. I can't believe that we did.'

The afternoon sun blazed down on them. There was no shade where they had landed, and it would be a long time before the sun set.

'Clara,' Polly said. 'I'm sorry for everything.'

'You've done nothing wrong. I'm the one who should be sorry. You're my best friend and I treated you abominably.'

'I betrayed you.'

'No, you didn't. Count Gregori . . . Anton . . . tells me that you behaved impeccably, and I believe he did too.' Clara reached and took Polly's hand, even though it clearly caused her pain to do so. 'I don't know how we can put this right, but I do know that I don't want to lose you as my friend.'

'Me neither,' said Polly.

Clara looked around. She was shivering and Polly feared she would go into shock before help came. 'This is where my mother and father died.'

'What? Oh, Clara, I am so sorry. I had no idea it was here.'

Clara nodded. 'Someone has been trying to kill us, haven't they? First you, then me. And Anton.'

'I think they needed to separate us, because they knew I would keep an eye on you.'

'Only two people would do such a thing,' Clara said. 'Only two people were set to gain if I died before I married. Only two people gained from my mother and father's death.'

'I know. Your aunt and uncle. It's wicked. Just wicked. It proves that you won't be safe until you are married. We have nothing to prove they did all this. If you wait four years, they will try again.'

'It will break your heart,' said Clara.

'It would break my heart if I lost you too,' Polly said, as a tear rolled down her cheek. 'Love is not just one thing or the other, Clara. My love for you as my friend is as deep as my romantic love for Anton. I would do anything to keep you safe.'

'At the cost of your own happiness?'

'It will hurt for a while, but I will be happy again one day. I'll be happy knowing they can't hurt you anymore.'

'Oh, Polly, I don't deserve you, I really don't.'

'Of course you do.'

'I've been so selfish. I've missed you.'

'Me too. You're my best friend.'

'We're more than friends. You know that. We're cousins.' When Clara saw Polly's surprise, she said. 'Oh, don't think I didn't know. He tormented my aunt with it all the time. I would have felt sorry for her, if she'd shown an ounce of humanity towards me and others.' Clara closed her eyes.

'Don't go to sleep, Clara. I need you

to stay awake until they come.'

'I'm so tired.'

'Please, stay awake. Tell me what you've been doing since I left.'

'I've been sitting in my room wishing you would come back and be my friend again,' Clara laughed, but it was weak. She tried to move, then cried out as her leg twisted painfully.

Polly lost track of how long it was before they heard a shout from below. She moved far enough to look down the cliff and saw a group of people there. She could only see the tops of their heads, but her heart flipped when she saw one head of thick, wavy hair.

'Are either of you hurt?' Someone called from below.

'I am alright, but I think my friend, Clara, has broken her leg!'

'Wait!' came the order. Anton and another man jumped on horses and started on the road to the mountain, while others watched.'

Another age later, there came a cry from above of 'Look out below!'

Someone was lowering a stretcher down. Meanwhile, someone else was climbing down, fixing a rope to the cliff every few yards. The stretcher came closer, until it was just above the girls' heads.

'We need to get you onto the stretcher,' Polly said. It had thick straps around it, so she could be fixed in securely. 'I don't know if I can manage to do all the straps from here. Or to lift you on.'

They struggled for a while, as Polly tried to get Clara under her arms, to ease her onto the stretcher. Every movement was agony for her friend, until beads of sweat ran down both their faces. Polly managed to get the top half of Clara's body onto the stretcher, but her legs were hanging over the side, and too far away for Polly to reach safely on the narrow ledge.

She was so intent on helping, she had barely paid attention to the climber, until he landed at the other end of the ledge, and she realised it was Anton.

'Wait,' he said to Polly who had been

trying to reach across Clara to help her. 'I'll help you. I'm sorry, Clara, but this is going to hurt.'

She screamed in pain when he caught her legs and pivoted them onto the stretcher. 'I'm sorry,' he said again, as he fixed the straps around her legs. She winced but did not cry out again. 'Ready, Mr Garibaldi!' he called to the man above. 'Polly, wait, and we'll come back for you,' he said.

They pulled the stretcher up, with Anton following at the side, to steady it whenever it teetered. The progress was slow and laborious. Every now and then, he had to help the stretcher traverse overhanging rocks and smaller ledges than the one they had landed on. Each time, Clara let out an involuntary cry of pain and frustration, but other than that, she did not complain.

Polly waited on the ledge, thirsty, hungry and frightened, but relieved that Clara would be safe. The sun felt hotter than ever, and her face began to burn.

Finally, she heard sound above her

and saw Anton coming back down the cliff face, much faster than before, because the ropes were already attached. He landed on the ledge, carrying what appeared to be a belt loop on his own belt.

'Can you stand?' he asked.

She nodded. Stand yes. Speak no. Her tongue and lips were parched and swollen.

He put his hand in his pocket and took out a flask. 'Here,' he said. 'Drink this.'

She took the flask from him and drank back the cool, fresh water.

'I'm sorry I didn't bring any the first time, but we feared that time was of the essence, with Clara's leg. The nuns brought the water.'

'Of course. Is she alright? You should have stayed with her.'

'I just had the same conversation with her about you, with the added threat that if I did not personally come back for you, she would curse my family for generations to come,' he said with a wry smile. 'How did I ever get involved with you two? I am not sure which one of you terrifies me most — or which one impresses me most.'

'You're a lucky man, that's what you are.'

He smiled and held out his hand. 'Come on, if you can stand.'

Polly was sure she could stand, until she tried it. Then her legs gave way and she fell against him. He put his arm around his waist with one hand, and took the spare belt off his with the other. She realised that the belts were actually joined with a loop, so that she was clasped extremely close to him. 'Put your arms around my neck,' he said.

She did as she was bid, and held on tight, finding her head lolling against his shoulder. She told herself it was exhaustion, when in fact it was relief and a longing for a warm connection. He had one arm around her waist, holding tight, and the other above him, holding the rope. She decided to enjoy the closeness while she could, because she might have to go away again.

He shouted, 'Now!' to whoever was above and they were suddenly lifted off the ledge and pulled up, inch by inch. She clung to him all the way, trying to memorise his male aroma and how his taut body felt pressed against hers. It was something she would be able to think about in the years to come, when she was alone and did not have to pretend not to care anymore.

After what seemed another lifetime, they were helped over the barrier. There were several people waiting there, including a stocky, suntanned man with grey hair and some of the nuns.

'There was a man,' Polly said.

'We've got him,' said Anton. 'But he won't talk about who hired him and the Lovett woman.'

'It was her aunt and uncle.'

'Of that I have no doubt.' He steadied her when it seemed as if she would topple over.

'Thank you, Mr Garibaldi,' Anton said, taking the man's hand, and shaking it warmly.

'Yes, thank you,' said Polly. Her legs were trembling but she moved away from the edge, convinced she would never want to visit the White Peak ever again. The nuns descended on her, and she found herself being spirited away from Anton, sustained only by the memory of him holding her tight.

27

The taxi dropped Lena and the children at the gate to her grandmother's cottage. It stood about a hundred yards from a cliff edge, overlooking the English Channel, and in the gardens of the hotel which fronted the road about another hundred yards further inland. In the distance, out over the sea, she could see planes flying over the coastline, practising for the coming war.

'Are you alright, Reuben?' she asked. 'And you, Rachel?'

'Yes, Mummy,' they both said.

Her heart swelled with love. She had not been able to leave them at the hospital while she travelled to Scarborough, even though she knew they were safe there. They had been abandoned enough. She vowed that would never happen again. The authorities had given her interim permission to keep them. They had other things to take care of, like the coming war, so she had done them a favour by taking responsibility for the twins.

She opened the gate and walked down the garden path, holding Rachel's hand on one side and Reuben's on the other. 'I grew up here,' she told them. 'More or less. My mother and father both worked long hours, so I spent a lot of time with my grandmother. I can't wait for you to meet her.'

'I can't wait to meet Polly Smith,' said Rachel. There had been a lot of discussion on the way about who she might be.

The front door was open, as if they had been expected. She went into the narrow hallway, with its forget-me-not wallpaper, and turned right into the cosy sitting room, with its chintz chairs and curtains. She could smell fresh bread and pastries. On the coffee table stood a Lazy Susan, filled to the brim with sandwiches, cakes and biscuits.

Her grandmother sat in her chair with her eyes closed, while four people stood with their backs to them, listening to the radio. The voice on the radio was the Prime Minister, declaring that Germany had invaded Poland and as such, Britain had no choice but to declare war. Even though it had been expected, everyone in the room took in a sharp breath.

'Are we at war now?' Rachel asked.

The four people turned around. It was Greg, his grandmother, Sister Dominique and the Count.

Bessie, ninety-three years old, opened her eyes. 'Lena, my Lena!'

Lena ran to her, kneeling down and hugging her. 'Nana, I want you to meet Rachel and Reuben. They're going to be staying with me . . . with us.' She glanced at Greg as she said it, with the unspoken gesture that this was his chance to escape while he could.

'Hello Rachel and Reuben,' Bessie said. 'Greg told me all about you. He said he had feeling you would be coming. I bet you're hungry. Children are always hungry. Have some cake, my little ducks. Take what you want. I baked them myself this morning. I want all those plates empty before they have to go back to the kitchen.'

The children needed no further encouragement. They had lived on half rations on the ship, and unappetising hospital food since they got to Britain. They all but dived on the food.

'Thank you,' Lena mouthed to her grandmother. She stood up.

'How did you know I was going to bring them?' she asked Greg.

'Because it was what I would have done,' he smiled. 'And don't forget you still owe me that dinner.'

'Sister Dominique? Or is that Polly Smith?'

'Oh, Lena,' her grandmother laughed. 'I thought I always told you that Polly had green eyes and Clara had blue eyes. I knew them straight away, even after all this time.'

'I don't understand,' Lena said. 'Polly Smith said she would be here. We felt sure it was Sister Dominique, hiding in plain sight.'

'And, so she is hiding in plain sight,' said the Countess, her green eyes flashing with humour. 'It was Sister Marie-Claire's idea in the end. While Clara and I were convalescing at the convent, she came to us and suggested that I take Clara's place at the wedding but that we put out the news that Clara had married. That way she would be safe from further assaults from her aunt and uncle.' The Countess put her arm in her husband's. 'I said I didn't even know if Anton wanted to marry me instead of Clara. Apparently Sister Marie Claire had taken care of that too.'

'I was given no choice,' said the Count with a smile that suggested he was happy to have been told what to do. 'If she'd had a shotgun, I am sure she would have brandished that. She was a remarkable woman. Terrifying, but remarkable.'

'I decided to take the veil and have been at the convent ever since,' said Sister Dominique. 'I am close there, to my parents.'

'You're Clara!' Lena said, as the last

piece of the jigsaw fell into place. 'And the Countess is Polly! All this time, and neither of you said anything.'

'We've kept our secret a long time,' said Clara. 'At first it was necessary, at least until my aunt and uncle died, then it became force of habit. Excuse the pun!' She pressed her hand to her wimple and laughed. 'But there was also the fact that the contract I had signed to marry Anton was legal and binding. We had broken that contract, though it has to be stressed that Polly and Anton are legally married in the eyes of God.'

'Didn't people know Clara looked different to Polly?' Rachel asked, through a mouthful of fruit cake. Once again, Lena blessed her for knowing exactly what to ask. She had no doubt that Rachel would make a great detective one day.

'Sister Marie Claire had a contingency plan for that too,' said the Countess. Lena would have to get used to thinking of her as Polly. 'She suggested we travel for a couple of years on an extended honeymoon. Then, by the time we returned, no one would remember what Clara Harrington looked like. And Sister Dominique — the real Clara — hardly left the convent for those two years. It did mean I had to cut off all ties with England. I'm so sorry I worried you, Bessie. I have thought about you, all the time.'

She knelt down at Bessie's feet and put her hand on Bessie's arm.

'I'm just glad I got to see you both again. I am so proud of you.' She reached out her other hand for Clara's — Sister Dominique's hand.

'And now,' said the Count, 'I have been able to ask the British government for help to take back Cariastan.'

'That was your mission from the King?' Lena asked.

'It was. I carried the treaty papers. That's why the Germans tried to stop us. I'm sorry I put us all in danger.'

'It's incredible,' said Lena, laughing. 'Absolutely incredible. My head is spinning. I think I need some fresh air.'

She left them all chatting while she

went out into the garden. She stood at the gate, thinking it all over. How lucky the three were to know a love and a friendship that had lasted for over fifty years. Polly and Clara had risen above all the challenges and, finally, made it back home to Bessie. Lena wiped away a stray tear.

'Here,' said a voice next to her. It was Greg. He handed her a handkerchief.

'You knew all along, you pig,' she said, grinning. 'You could have just said, 'Oh by the way, my grandmother is Polly and she married Anton'. Or Gregori, or whatever his name is, and Clara took the veil.'

'Just call me Scheherazade,' he quipped. 'I didn't want to give too much away at once. I had to find some excuse to keep you interested in talking to me.'

'Actually, I would have been interested anyway. I understand though, if things are different now that I am taking on the children. It's a lot to consider. Especially with the war starting. Who knows how long it will last or where we will be when it's all over? I suppose you'll be returning home as soon as possible.' 'You're not trying to get out of our dinner, are you?' She turned to him and grabbed him by the lapels, bringing his lips down to hers.

'I consider it a legal and binding contract,' she whispered, before pressing her mouth against his.

28

The *Caria* sailed into the calm waters just off Cariastan. Polly stood at the deck, holding a tiny bundle in her arms. Anton stood behind her, with his arms around her waist.

'Home at last,' he said, kissing her gleaming red hair.

'You don't regret leaving, do you?' she asked. 'I sometimes worry you had no say in any of this. It was all decided for you.'

She turned to face him. Most of the time, she just thanked her lucky stars that he was her husband, but sometimes she worried and thought about what his life might have been with a wife who was not so much beneath him in status.

He stroked her smooth cheek, and then the equally smooth cheek of the beautiful bundle she carried.

'All this,' he said. 'Is exactly what I would have chosen. I love you, Countess de Luca, and don't you forget it. I have loved you since we first sailed on this ship. I have loved you since you came out of the bedroom at Derwent and dropped petticoats at my feet. I would not have shamed Clara or let her down, but in my heart, I knew that you and I were meant to be together. So, no, it was not all decided for me. At least not by Sister Marie-Claire, although I think that if she'd had a shotgun, she would have used it!

'A much higher power meant for us to be together, and Clara was the one who made it all happen. A rather reluctant fairy godmother, but one nonetheless. I shall be forever grateful for her unselfish heart. I love you, and I can never regret the road that led to that.'

He pulled her gently into his arms, so as not to crush the baby, and kissed her.

The boat finished docking, and they saw a figure in a nun's habit waiting on the quayside for them.

'Come on,' she said, her heart filled with love. 'Let's introduce our son to his fairy godmother.'